And Love Replied

Other Books by Mary Stolz

And

Love

Replied

by Mary Stolz

PERENNIAL LIBRARY

HARPER & ROW, PUBLISHERS

NEW YORK AND EVANSTON

AND LOVE REPLIED was originally published by Harper & Brothers in 1958. First PERENNIAL LIBRARY edition published 1964 by Harper & Row, Publishers, Incorporated, New York and Evanston.

LIBRARY OF CONGRESS CATALOG CARD NUMBER: 58-9781

H–O

TO
ALASTAIR REID

And Love Replied

1

THE MOVERS GAVE A LAST LOOK around, slammed the truck doors, climbed in the cab and started away, giving perfunctory waves. They were Chicago movers, and they were going back to Chicago. The Wilders, who were also from Chicago but now a long way from it, gazed after them wistfully.

They looked about the living room of their new house with misgiving. There was so much to do. There were so many barrels and boxes and suitcases and piles of books. So many bleak, uncurtained windows. It seemed useless to make any start toward order. Mrs. Wilder said she didn't recognize half the things she saw.

"They must have moved somebody else's things."

"We should have stayed where we were," her husband said accusingly, but his wife and daughter refused to accept any responsibility.

"You're the one who got transferred," Mrs. Wilder said. "I can do housework anywhere."

"And I'd rather have finished school where I was," Betty said.

He looked at them glumly. "Let's go out and get something to eat."

Mrs. Wilder vetoed that promptly. "Oh, no. We'll have to get things somewhat to rights here first. I'll fix us a sandwich or something."

"Surely we didn't pack bread?"

"I'll open a can of beans. We can go out for dinner, I suppose, but we have"—she glanced at her watch—"we have a good four hours before dinnertime, and we'd better make the most of them."

Mr. Wilder and Betty knew when there would be more energy expended in escaping a job than in doing it. Without much grace, they agreed to help make the most of the time.

"Let's see, now," Mrs. Wilder said slowly. "Dishes and bedrooms first, of course." She looked yearningly at the vacant windows. "I'd adore to get those washed and the curtains ironed and hung before we go to bed."

"Mother, please," Betty protested. "We'll be up all night."

"I didn't say I was going to, dear. I only said I wanted to." Her longing tone altered to a practical one. "Well then . . . Betty, you'd best unpack the dishes while your father helps me move furniture in the bedrooms. No point worrying about the guest room today, I suppose. But yours and ours will have to be done. And then I'll make beds and unpack linen, and you," she said to her husband, "can get to work in here on the books. We won't be able to move until that clutter is out of the way, and then when that's done—"

"Done?" Mr. Wilder said loudly. "I won't be done for hours."

"You will if you put them away without reading them."

"But I want to get them properly arranged. It'll take thought, and time, and—"

"Arrange them later, dear. Just get them on the shelves for today."

"That's what we said last time we moved, and they never got arranged at all, and since the last time we moved was shortly after we got married and that was almost nineteen years ago, I've been living nineteen years with my books arranged all wrong. I'd prefer to start right, this time."

Mrs. Wilder considered. "I'll tell you what. You get them out of the way today, and I'll help with the rearrangement whenever you want me to."

Mr. Wilder brightened, and his daughter smiled. Once the books were on the shelves there wasn't a chance that he would face the task of taking them all out again for a proper job of sorting. But he seemed quite happy.

"Fine," said Mrs. Wilder blandly. "Now, Betty, I think it would be best if after you got the everyday dishes washed you call me and I'll help—"

"Do I have to wash them?" Betty interrupted. "Why wash them? They've only been traveling in their little cartons. I mean, it isn't as if they'd been out doing a day's work, or anything, that would get them dirty."

"They've been wrapped in newspaper," Mrs. Wilder said in a firm, patient voice. "We don't want to start in our new house with dirty dishes on the shelves."

"Couldn't we wash them as we go along?"

Mrs. Wilder stood, hands on her hips, surveying her family. "Now, both of you, listen. I'll get little enough work from you once we've settled in, but I do intend to have help this weekend. You'll be gone next week," she said to her husband, "and Betty will be starting school pretty soon and using that as an excuse to get out of everything she possibly can, so the only thing *I* can do is work you both while I have the chance. Which I am going to do." She sounded determined.

"Okay," Betty said, getting up with a sigh. "I wash them." She turned at the door to the dining room. "Come and let's look at our back yard for a minute."

Together the three of them walked to a window facing their new back yard. It was small, but it had a great drooping willow in one corner, and the grass was green and neat. Beyond the yard was a reach of meadow, at the far end of which the railroad ran. A red and silver train, looking small in the distance, sped past as they stood there.

Mr. Wilder, turning his head, studied the grass a moment. "That's odd. Somebody mowed. Who could have done that?"

"The Blairs?" his wife asked.

"They moved out of here two weeks ago. That was mowed yesterday or today."

"Maybe they left instructions."

Mr. Wilder, who'd bought the house from the Blairs, shook his head. "I was lucky to get the lawn at all." His curiosity aroused, he went back to the living room and said, "By gosh, the front's been done, too. Mysterious."

"Oh, well," Mrs. Wilder said, dismissing the lawns as time-consuming, "probably some neighborhood boy did it on speculation. We'll find out soon enough. Funny we didn't notice it before."

"We've been too busy."

Betty had wandered disconsolately into the kitchen, and her mother now followed, sending a practiced eye around the room, taking in shelves and cupboards. All was immaculate.

The three Wilders had arrived in town the evening before, and had spent several hours of darkness cleaning. They'd passed the night in a motel and had been on their new doorstep, Mrs. Wilder filled with enterprise, Betty and her father stifling yawns, when the van arrived. All the while the movers trudged back and forth in what seemed to Betty the easier part of the job, the Wilders scrubbed and polished and rinsed away the Blairs, who, Betty decided, were already so clean as to be quite self-effacing.

"I've come to the conclusion," she said to her father at one point, waving hands mittened with soapsuds, "that only messy people can leave their imprint behind. I mean, you can leave your footprint on the sands of time, or even on the dust of time, but how can you leave it on the clean tile floor of time?"

Mr. Wilder grinned. "So endeth the Blairs . . . in an eddy of detergent."

"Well, dear," Mrs. Wilder said now, "you might as well get started. The everyday dishes are here, in this

4

barrel. Nice and convenient to the dishwasher. This won't be any job at all. Just stack the dishes in the washer—not the silver, mind, you'll have to do that by hand—and while one load is washing you can unpack another. Try not to break anything."

Mrs. Wilder had a tendency to admonitions of this sort. She told her husband, each time he left for a trip on the road, to be sure to drive carefully. She instructed Betty, at examination time, to do her best. She advised both of them to eat properly, not to catch cold, to wear nice underwear all the time so as not to be ashamed of what they had on when they got to the hospital. She told Betty not to talk to strangers, her husband not to give them rides. She tried, it appeared to her husband and daughter, to cover all contingencies, and had a rather touching faith in the power of words to avert trouble.

Having done what she could for her everyday dishes, she beckoned her husband upstairs, leaving Betty about to protest that she had no idea how to run the dishwasher.

"Mother?"

But she hadn't spoken loudly, and their footsteps on the uncarpeted stairs, their voices discussing the disposition of beds, covered her call completely. Oh, well. Any nincompoop could load the thing. Time enough to call for further instructions when she had it filled.

In Chicago they hadn't had a dishwasher. They hadn't had a house. Betty in her life had only known an apartment, and this house so fascinated her that she almost didn't mind having to spend her final year of high school in a strange town, among strangers. That they would not remain strangers all year was of no particular comfort now, when she knew no single soul.

But . . . put that out of mind. The unknown school, the unknown people and streets that lay ahead. Put out of mind, also, everything and everyone that was behind, or the next thing you knew you'd be in tears. Put from mind Carol, her best friend, and George, whom she hadn't loved but almost had, and the lake and the Loop. Forget, for the time being, all that, because it could only make you miserable. Here you were, and inescap-

5

ably, in a suburban town outside New York, living in a house that had a dishwasher and stairs and a front and back yard and a meadow beyond. Ordinary enough matters for lots of people, but entrancing to some who had never known them.

Anyway, she thought, unwrapping dishes, stacking them in the machine, scattering newspapers in a wide litter so her mother would have something to exclaim about, anyway, I'll be all right in this school, this town. No need to get exercised. Streets and unfamiliar school buildings are easy enough to get used to. As for the people—teachers and students—why, they *are* just people. I've always gotten along all right with people. Haven't I? Yes, I have.

She shook her head, reminding herself she'd determined not to think on these problems.

The dishwasher was really rather marvelous. The way the different-sized plates and things fitted in as if on purpose. Well, it was on purpose, of course. It had been designed that way . . . so that the saucer just slid in here, and the salad plates in there. Too bad Mother felt silver couldn't be done in the thing.

Carol, who also coped with dishes for her family, didn't have a dishwasher. She'd be limp with envy when she heard. Newspapers rose around Betty like a paper hill, and she fitted dishes into their niches and wondered what Carol was doing now. Sleeping, probably. It was an hour earlier in Chicago than here, and Carol was one of the most relentless Saturday sleepers of Betty's acquaintance. "Saves talking to the family," she'd say lightly. And George? Betty's lips curved fondly. George, unquestionably, was in his laboratory. His bedroom, really. But George, who was going to be an entomologist, had fitted it up like a comic-strip scientist's dream. Slides and retorts and charts of unthinkably horrible insects. "Do *not* call them bugs," she heard him implore. "A six-legged creature is an insect. Do you know that technically even a lobster is an insect and not a fish at all?" "No," she'd replied, "but now that you tell me, I'm glad I don't like to eat the things." He had dozens of jars of horrors and a really fine microscope, into whose strange world she had peered, at his bidding, with interest and confusion, for nearly a year.

"What are you doing, at this very moment?" she asked him in her mind.

"Thinking of you, Betty. Missing you so."

She frowned a bit at this insincere-sounding answer, changed it to "Trying to get a plant louse to lie on its side."

Yes, that was more like George, who had almost loved her, but was driven by ambition's spur, and would remember her affectionately, between insects. Any rotifer wriggling, she thought now, could take his mind off me. Any paramecium replace me, any amoeba pale my image.

Only, I wasn't going to think of these things.

Now I live in a house, in Norwood, which is fifty miles from New York City, a fairly easy commute and practically like the country. Look at that meadow out there. When did you ever expect to look out of your own kitchen window and see a weeping willow tree and a meadow, and—she leaned over the sink with surprise and pleasure—and a *horse?*

A heavy brown horse was ambling across the meadow, stretching his long neck down to nibble grass, lifting to contemplate the scene about him, stopping to rub awhile along the fence, moving on. Shiny, easygoing, a very nice horse, he succeeded in ousting Chicago from Betty's thoughts. She leaned on the sink, watching him dreamily, and wondered where he came from, what he did for a living. What's a horse's place in modern society? A nice bridle horse, now. That was one thing. But this fellow, with his enormous flanks, his huge head, his thick legs . . . he ought to be pulling a cart. Except, are there any carts left to pull? I thought everything went on gasoline these days.

"Betty, what *are* you doing?"

She straightened at her mother's voice, turned and smiled. "Watching this horse."

"Horse?" said her mother, coming forward. She looked out the window. "So there is. What in the world do you suppose he's for?"

They stood staring, as though neither had ever seen a

horse before, until Mrs. Wilder recollected herself. "Betty," she said hopelessly, "just look at those papers scattered around. Why *will* you make more work?"

"I didn't know what to do with them."

"You didn't have to scatter them all over the place this way. Stuff them into one of those boxes over there, and we can burn them later. Let's see—" She studied the interior of the dishwasher. "That's about as much as you can get in, I suppose."

Betty supposed so, too.

"Well, now," said her mother, "where's the detergent? Here . . . Now watch what I do, so you'll know. A little bit in this slot here, and press the lid down, and turn this, and there we are."

"Where?" said Betty, when the machine remained silent.

"That's funny." Mrs. Wilder sprang the lid open, closed it again, turned the knob. Nothing happened. "It's *broken*," she wailed. "Oh, wouldn't you just know! . . . It worked perfectly when Mrs. Blair showed me that time. What can be the *matter* with it?"

"I don't know."

"Don't be difficult, Betty. You'd better call your father."

"I don't think he'll know either."

"He can decide what to do. Here the *phone* isn't even in. Oh, dear. Well, you'll just have to do them by hand after all—"

"Wait'll I call Daddy," Betty said hastily, and fled. Not that there was any escaping the fact. Whether or not Daddy managed to get someone to fix the dishwasher, Betty was going to have to do all those things by hand, because it would be ages before help came, probably, and her mother was not one to stand around waiting while it did.

Oh, murder, she said to herself. "Daddy!" she called up the stairs, and then started up them. "Daddy, the dishwasher is broken."

Her father came out of a bedroom, holding a lamp. "Where does this go?"

"Downstairs. In the living room."

"How did it get up here?"

"I don't know. The moving men, probably. Maybe it'd look nice in the guest room. It's not really a living-roomy lamp."

Mr. Wilder revolved it in front of him. "Nice, though. Well, let's try it in there."

They went into the guest room, which faced front (the Wilders having taken the two back bedrooms in order to see the meadow when they woke), and Mr. Wilder put the lamp on a bedside table. "Too big?" he asked doubtfully.

"Try it on that table over there instead."

"That's an idea." He started across the room.

"What are you two doing?" Mrs. Wilder's voice came up the stairs reproachfully. "Can't I depend on either one of you? I'm down here with this broken machine. What are you *doing?*"

"What broken machine?" Mr. Wilder shouted.

"Oh, for goodness' sake! Come down, please. We can't keep yelling this way."

"What's broken?" Mr. Wilder asked his daughter.

"The dishwasher."

"Broken how?"

"It won't go."

"Oh."

They descended to the kitchen in silence, and in silence Mr. Wilder approached the dishwasher, peered inside, jiggled the lid. He turned to his wife. "What seems to be the matter with it?"

"It seems to not go."

"I wonder," he said, after a pause, "if anyone really knows in what contempt I hold machines."

It's apparently reciprocal, Betty thought, but decided not to say anything. Perhaps, though he didn't admit it, her father was secretly ashamed of his inability to master any mechanical device. Even can-openers balked him, so what could he do with something the size of this dishwasher?

But, if he couldn't cope himself, he almost invariably had the name of someone who could. "Let's see, now," he was muttering. "Somewhere or other I have the name of that fellow Blair spoke of. You remember," he said to his wife. "He told us at the closing. Young man

9

who lives around here somewhere and can fix anything built by the human hand."

"I remember something like that. Look in your wallet."

Mr. Wilder got out his wallet, leafed through it, extracted a piece of paper. "Knew I had it. Where are my glasses?"

Mrs. Wilder took it from him. "Clifton Banks, Bolt's Hollow." She glanced up. "Where or what is Bolt's Hollow?"

"A road, just down the way a bit. Maybe I'd better take a run over and see if I can find him."

"Why don't you call a plumber? Or would it be an electrician?"

"I wouldn't know. Blair said, whatever goes wrong, get hold of young Banks. He's better than anyone else in town, and handier, and cheaper. Blair says you could be holding your finger in the dike for six months before one of the local plumbers came round to plug it up for you and then he'd charge for a gold plug. It isn't one bit different in Chicago, I told him. Plumbers and electricians have inherited the earth, and the rest of us are here on sufferance, to provide burnt-out fuses and stopped-up sinks—"

"I'm sorry to interrupt," said Mrs. Wilder, "and I'd like to have you go into this at length some other time, but don't you think you'd better go along and see if you can get Mr. Banks? We have all these dishes to do, and I don't suppose Betty is longing to do them by hand."

"She isn't," Betty said. "Not in the least. Mother, we can leave these in, can't we? I mean, if this man lives so close and behaves so handy, maybe it'll be done in just a few minutes."

"Whatever happened to the adverb?" Mr. Wilder asked her. "Hasn't anyone mentioned adverbs to you in school?"

Betty laughed. "School is about the only place you ever do hear one mentioned."

"Or used, I suppose," Mr. Wilder said morosely. He added to his wife, "And only a moment ago you split an infinitive. Well . . . I'm off. Hope I find the fellow in."

When he'd gone, Mrs. Wilder suggested to Betty that she come upstairs and help put away linens. They were in the midst of this job when they heard the car return.

"Hello, hello," Mr. Wilder called. "We're in luck. Young Banks will be right over. And what do you think? He's the one who mowed our lawn. A neighborly gesture, he says, and I didn't know how to thank him, neighbors being what they are in Chicago. Neighborly is the right word, too, in all senses. I drove to Bolt's Hollow, and it turns out to be right around the corner, you could walk it in a minute. He's walking now. Just stopped to get his tools, and said he'd—"

Mrs. Wilder put aside a pile of sheets. "I'd better go down," she said. "He'll stand there shouting until I do. Are you coming?"

"No point, is there? I'll go on with this, and if he gets the dishwasher fixed, I'll go on with that. It's just going to be work of some kind or another all week end anyway, isn't it?"

"That's about it," said her mother cheerfully.

Betty, piling pillow cases, did not reply.

"Betty?"

"What is it?"

"Doesn't it seem a pity to start sulking over work the very first day in our new house?"

Betty wavered on the verge of asking what difference it made if she sulked here or in Chicago, work was work, and then changed her mind. In a curious way, she agreed with her mother. It was a new home, a house that had stairs within and a meadow outside. It could be a new sort of start. "Sorry," she muttered.

Mrs. Wilder hesitated, hand on the newel post. "Well . . . I'll go down." She went, slowly at first, and then more quickly, to see what her husband was doing.

Mother often leaves me that way, Betty thought, moving on to the pile of sheets. As if she were first reluctant, and then released. She supposed, in a detached way, that it was because she did sulk so much—about housework, that was. Otherwise, she was quite pleasant and accommodating, and she got along with her parents better than most people she knew. Carol or George, for instance. (They didn't get along with their parents at all, and so weren't good examples.) But, better than lots of people.

But the pressure of housework, that always seemed so futile, that could never be avoided (or hardly ever), that took up so much time better spent doing practically anything else, threw her into a rebellious despondency that probably did look like sullenness.

Not for me, she thought, hearing the sound of what was no doubt Mr. Banks's footstep on the back porch, and then his voice in the kitchen. Not for me. (A nice voice, she registered, with that part of her mind not engaged in grim programing for the future. A young voice.) She got back to the matter in hand. When I'm . . . not that silly word grown-up, I'm grown-up now . . . when I'm independent, earning my own living, I will earn it in such a way as to dispose of housekeeping altogether. I'll be a journalist, running around the world, eating in peculiar restaurants, living in odd quarters. I'll risk food poisoning, rather than cook my own meals, and live in strange rooms under strange skies my whole life long before I'll submit to counting how many handkerchiefs the laundry lost this week and catching that fluff of dust the vacuum didn't reach. I'll be an archaeologist, or a Navy nurse, or a traveling salesman, like Daddy. But a housewife I will not be.

Why did so many girls settle for home and husband?

"They can call it love if they want to," Betty had once said to Carol. "I call it madness."

"Don't be silly," Carol had said calmly. "The fact that most girls want what you don't doesn't constitute madness in them."

"In me, then?"

"Not necessarily. Just a difference. Anyway, you don't want to be all those things because you want to be them. You only want not to be a housewife, which is quite a different matter. Ambition isn't part of it. Why don't you marry a rich man? That would settle your problem nicely."

But Betty felt that to dream of marrying riches in order to keep a stately distance between you and the Bendix was dishonest, and even a little creepy. According to tradition, girls who married for that reason lived miserably ever after. Like most people of seventeen, Betty was a traditionalist.

No, she thought now, straightening and moving away from the piles of linen, I shall earn freedom from drudgery myself, and in that way be able to enjoy it. But meanwhile and just the same and nevertheless, it *would* be a good idea, maybe, to put a better face on it while escape is impossible.

Okay. I'll put a better face on it. Now what? Well, now she could probably go down and express an interest in the dishwasher. Not that she was not interested. She regarded the dishwasher very highly as a going mechanism; it was how it got fixed that was unimportant.

There was a sudden tremendous hum from the lower regions of the house.

"Well, I'll be darned," she heard her father say. "You actually did it."

Mr. Banks's reply, if there was one, was inaudible, but, recalling his voice, Betty sped into her room to run a brush through her hair and apply a little lipstick to her work-wan mouth before going downstairs.

"All fixed?" she asked, coming into the kitchen with the quick sweet smile, the airy walk, the heightened sensibility that automatically took possession of her in the new presence of any young man. Sometimes, when the object seemed worthy and challenging, it remained and was part of her. But always, until this moment, it was an attitude of which she was aware. You held your head so, you moved and lifted and dropped your eyes thus, you put into your voice something it was innocent of in the sole presence of your family, say, or of Carol. If the boy was dull, or obviously chartered by someone else, if no slightest current moved between you and him, why, you tucked the whole pleasant pantomime away, not because it was artificial, but because it served no purpose.

13

Faced with Clifton Banks, all the pretty, self-conscious airs fell from her like misty imaginings in a ray of strong truth. He had the oldest young face she had ever seen. Already lined, with eyes a little drawn, he had an expression—honest and unguarded—that belonged on the face of someone far younger. Betty thought he was eighteen, maybe nineteen. Too old to look so open. That it was also the handsomest face she had ever seen was almost beside the point.

"Clifton Banks," said Mrs. Wilder. "My daughter, Betty."

They nodded, looked away from each other, and both began to talk to Mr. Wilder.

"That about does it," said Clifton Banks, as Betty said, "Isn't it wonderful it's fixed?"

They stopped, apologized, laughed slightly and fell silent.

What should I call him? Betty wondered. He's too young to be called Mr. Banks. But . . . Clifton? It was the first time she'd ever thought it might be forward to call a boy by his first name.

Capable and tall, sleeves rolled up on his brown arms, he assembled his tools in a battered old metal box and was clearly not prepared to linger. Does he go to the high school? Betty wondered. Or maybe he'd be finished. That box of his, it looks awfully used. Is he a handyman in the summer, to earn money? How old *is* he?

Mr. Wilder reached into his pocket.

"No, that's all right, sir," Clifton Banks said.

"Well, now, look, you did our lawn, and now you've made the machine go, and I just can't accept—"

"It's okay, really."

"But—"

Clifton Banks flushed. It made, Betty noted, his blue eyes sky-like. "This was no job at all," he said. "The thing wasn't broken, it was just acting silly. As for the lawn, I happened to have the mower out and it was beginning to look like a wheatfield over here. You'd have needed a scythe."

"I don't know how to thank you."

"No need." He picked up his box, nodded to Betty without looking at her, thrust his hand out abruptly to Mrs. Wilder. "Bye, ma'am. Good-by, sir."

"We'll be seeing you again, won't we?" Mrs. Wilder said.

"Oh, sure. I'm around and about. Let me know if you get in any trouble."

"Not if we can't—" Mr. Wilder began. "That is, I certainly don't want to have you doing this sort of thing for—" He broke off, unable to decide how to put his thought.

"That's okay," said Clifton Banks at the back door. "After today we can consider it a business arrangement." He was gone, leaving the three Wilders to regard one another with that air of pleased discovery that follows the meeting of someone it would be pleasant to meet again.

Only Mrs. Wilder, who tended to look upon every encounter as one that might produce a friend, voiced this opinion. "What a nice person," she said.

"Seems to be," said her husband, who usually claimed he knew enough people and the last thing he required was additional acquaintance.

Betty said nothing.

That he'd all but ignored her, scarcely included her in his good-by, was not important. She decided, as she usually did when a boy seemed distant in her presence, that he was shy.

I'll never forget the first time I saw him, she thought. For the rest of my life I'll be able to look back and remember how it was. That it was late summer, late afternoon, and that I did not know how to speak to him, what to call him. That I forgot the flirty airs I never had to remember before. She tried to recall where she had first met George. In the chemistry lab? No . . . in some other classroom. Or on the school grounds? She couldn't quite recall. Nor what the weather had been like, nor what she'd thought of him. She rememered that he had responded to her immediately, and so—as this response will—fixed himself in her mind. I notice what they think of me, not what I think of them. That always comes later.

I have no idea what Clifton Banks thinks of me, but I have never seen anyone before that I wanted so much to see again. That I wanted so much to know.

2

THE PUBLISHING COMPANY FOR which Mr. Wilder was a book salesman had given him a week in which to move and settle in his new home. When the week was up, he left for a visit to the home office and a swing around his new territory.

"This house is sort of isolated," he said uncomfortably, the night before his departure. He and his wife were sitting in the living room, and Betty was upstairs, writing letters, she'd said.

The house was settled, as if they'd lived there for years, yet still with an air of freshness, unfamiliarity. That it was isolated, in a sense, was true. Particularly would it seem so to people who had come from a city apartment building. Like three bees who had left the hive and taken up residence in a meadow, they buzzed uncertainly and wondered what came next. A field with a horse and a distant railroad behind them, an unpaved road in front, a scattering of houses, distantly placed, around them. To the Wilders it spelled remoteness.

"A little late to consider that," Mrs. Wilder said good-humoredly.

Too good-humoredly, her husband decided. He had a tendency to think people were making the best of things when they were actually just contented.

"You nervous?" he asked.

"Not at all. Simply unaccustomed. We'll get used to it, if you don't scare us." She laughed. "You'd think we'd settled on the frontier, to hear you. This is a suburb, or an exurb. Anyway, it isn't an outpost."

"So long as the mails go through," he muttered, not entirely appeased. You went where your work took you, and a house had seemed a good thing after so many years of what they had termed, unoriginally but justifiably, a rabbit warren. Now he felt overwhelmed by thoughts of grass and snow and storm windows, all of which would have to be coped with, none of which he was sure he *could* cope with. And much of the time he wouldn't even be here. It had been all right, if not pleasant, to leave his wife and daughter alone in an apartment. But here?

"There's young Banks, of course," he said, looking through the walls in the direction of the Bankses' large house. An unhandsome, cumbersome place, but kept in wonderful repair. Presumably by Clifton, who seemed capable of keeping any number of large houses in good repair and perfect running order. "I wonder what he does."

"Works," said Mrs. Wilder promptly.

"Yes, but at what? What does he do especially?"

"He seems to be a carpenter, a plumber, a mechanic, a builder, a gardener, an electrician. I don't know what he does especially, except all of them."

"How do you know that?"

"I walked down this afternoon to that fruit stand his mother keeps on the highway. I bought corn and apples and then we talked a bit. I must say I did most of the talking, but Clifton went by in that pickup he drives, with a load of lumber on it, and I asked what he did, and Mrs. Banks said he could do anything. I quite believe it, I told her, and mentioned our lawn and the washing machine. She didn't seem *very* pleased. He'd never said anything about it, or about us."

"Not the talkative type."

"No . . . but, well, anyway, she knew we were here, of course, by the movers and the van and all, but not from Clifton. She says she hasn't time to call on us. She's busy most of the day at the fruit stand, and when she isn't there she's home canning and pickling things to sell, or tending her garden or doing her housework. She's not an awfully friendly woman. Not unfriendly, but too busy for people, you know. They make me feel terribly indolent. They must work all the *time*."

"You do enough," he said absently. "Is Betty going to like it here? Is she up there writing to Carol all this time because she's lonely, or homesick for Chicago? Or just because she wants to write?"

"Don't worry so much. Betty will be fine. Why shouldn't she be?"

And why, indeed, should she not? Betty was a girl who should get along no matter where you put her. She was so extraordinarily pretty and fresh-looking, so bright and—people often remarked on it—so sweet. And she was an optimist, a marvelous thing to be. How could Betty not care for life here, since where you were liked you were happy, and clearly Betty would be liked anywhere?

Still, tonight he was uneasy, leaving the two of them, his wife and daughter, so far from what they continued to call home. "Fits better than it did at home," Mr. Wilder would say, laying the old dining-room rug on the new dining-room floor, and Betty and her mother would agree, not noticing how he'd put it.

Well, he said to himself now, there's no help for it. We're here, and we'll have to make the best of it. He was oddly comforted by the thought of Clifton Banks nearby. A fellow who could obviously cope with anything from recalcitrant dishwashers to floods or wandering bears. Interesting, how some people had that immediate air of sufficiency, of authority even, regardless of age.

"How old is Banks?" he asked.

"Nineteen, his mother says."

"She should know."

"My, you're testy tonight."

"No, I'm not. I just don't like leaving you two. But you call him if anything goes wrong."

"You have a lot of faith in him."

"Yes. He has that air, you know."

"He has that. His father died when he was in his second year of high. Clifton quit school and went to work," she said with the careful intonation of a messenger arriving to say the battle has been lost.

"Quit school?" he exclaimed in just the tone of horror she'd expected. "That's perfectly awful."

"But none of our affair," she reminded him gently.

"It's everybody's affair when a person of that caliber has to leave school because of economic pressures. Society should hang its head. And don't tell me I'm not my brother's keeper. Half the trouble with the world is that no one will be his brother's keeper."

"Dear," said Mrs. Wilder, "his mother says he couldn't wait to quit. He hated school."

"A boy that bright? That gifted? I don't believe it. He could be a first-class engineer or scientist—"

"His mother says he hated school," Mrs. Wilder repeated, adding, "She should know."

"Never heard of such a thing in my life," Mr. Wilder grumbled. "How can a boy in his second year of high school know what he wants?"

"Clifton seems to know what he's doing. He has that air, you know."

"Stop repeating everything I say."

"Sorry." After a pause, Mrs. Wilder said, "The fact remains that you can't get her to do any housework without beating her on the head."

"Fact remains after what?" he said in a puzzled voice.

"After all the excellent human relations that she has. People like her, and she likes people, and life is very livable with Betty around, but it doesn't get her room straightened up, and it leaves us fighting over the dishes every night."

"She does them eventually, doesn't she?"

"Not always. And often well past her bedtime."

Mrs. Wilder was annoyed with herself for having started, once again, along this well-traveled groove. The trouble is, she thought gloomily, that it never seems possible to stop mid-groove, so to speak. Having started, you simply had to plod along till you came to the end. She heard herself going into the matter of Betty's messy bureau drawers, Betty's intransigence where marketing was concerned ("Over and over she comes home and says she *forgot*. I give her lists, I remind her, I do everything but tie a string around her finger, but she forgets—"), Betty's obvious lack of cooperation this past week.

"Do you think she did her share around here, helping us get settled?" she demanded.

Mr. Wilder looked thoughtful. You might have thought he was reviewing the week for the purpose of giving a reasoned answer. His wife knew he was merely seeking some evasion. And there . . . he'd found it. "She's done the dishes all right, hasn't she?"

"Well, with a *dishwasher*—" Mrs. Wilder broke off. "I'm boring myself," she said.

"I'd rather have her get along with people anyway, wouldn't you? More meaningful than tidy closets, or whatever."

"Oh, really!"

But it was hopeless, arguing with either of them. The truth was, Mrs. Wilder had not completely convinced herself that Betty's hatred of housework, her dreaminess, her occasional downright laziness, spelled an irrevocably flawed character. Maybe I'm wrong, she thought, examining the nature of housework. Something that had to be done over and over, monotonously, doggedly, and to what end? To no end. To renewed beginnings, always. On the other hand, housework was one of the fundamental disciplines of life. What would the world be if all its housewives decided that the vacuum cleaner and the pantry shelf and the kitchen stove were unmeaningful? A pigsty in which everyone was starving, that's what it would be, she told herself with some satisfaction. Perhaps as Betty grew older, she would learn that some disciplines (likable or not) were necessary. Didn't everyone have to learn that?

"Let's look at Wyatt Earp," Mr. Wilder suggested, and yawned.

Mrs. Wilder, happily relinquishing a useless line of thought, agreed.

In her room, Betty sat at her desk, looking out the window. The letter to Carol, begun an hour earlier, lay before her.

"Dear Carol: City living has eaten shamefully into our moral fiber, I am sad to say. Deprived of elevators, incinerators, and drugstore deliveries, we crouch in our cave, wondering how to fend off tigers. . . ."

She certainly had more than that to say to Carol (and somehow, written down, it didn't seem so very amusing, though the idea had seemed silly and bright enough before she'd started), but nerveless, limpid, almost without thought, she'd laid down her pen, fixed her eyes on the darkening meadow, and so had remained ever since. Over to the left the great bulk of the Banks house was unlighted save for the kitchen windows. It was too far away to see any movement within, but Betty was not interested, since the driveway was empty. At noon, through her own kitchen window, she had seen the pickup truck arrive, and Clifton Banks, in dungarees and red plaid shirt, swing lightly (for all his height) out and in through the back door.

That was as much as she'd seen of him during the entire week. Driving by in his truck, pulling into his driveway in his truck.

She knew the sound of that truck as soon as it turned off the highway, heading toward Bolt's Hollow. She knew when it stood, filling the driveway, filling the world, announcing for all who wished to know (Only me? she wondered. Does he have a girl somewhere? More than one? None at all—or more than one, she prayed) that Clifton Banks, wherever he had been, was now home, moving around in those rooms, available to his mother, should she wish to speak to him, available to anyone who wanted to phone or drop by.

Except me, she thought. Except me.

Nothing was as empty as that driveway when the truck was away, nothing as beatingly alive as the sight of its battered bulk parked there at the back door. For me, it might just as well be in Tibet, she thought. Her eyes dropped to her letter.

Suppose I wrote, "Dear Carol: I am in love with a truck, madly. I wait for it, watch for it, weave my girlish dreams and my life around it, and this truck doesn't know I'm alive. . . ."

Elbows on the desk, chin resting on her fists, she sighed and felt her heart begin to thud, as if it knew the time. In a little while, if he was on schedule, if the past three nights had not been accidentally timed, the truck would appear and this tense, tight sense of waiting would go. She would know—for a while—where he was.

She couldn't tell Carol anything of this. Carol would say this was physical attraction. "*How* handsome?" she'd say. "And you spoke to him once? That's biology, not sentiment, dear." But Carol would be wrong. Handsome he was, but she had fallen in love with more than his looks. I'm in love with his presence, the sense of him, the fact of him. He's different and wonderful, and I *could* know all that at one meeting. I could, because I did.

Night continued to fill a sky long emptied of day. There'd been endless twilights this week, and nothing to call sunsets. Day left, night came, like a couple of policemen exchanging duty. In just a little while now . . .

"Dear Carol: I wish I had never left Chicago, because at last I have fallen in love and it isn't what we thought at all, it just consists of looking at a truck. . . ."

They used to talk of it at length, the two of them. Settled in Carol's room or her own, they'd abandon the pretense of doing homework, to speculate on what it would be like, really being in love.

"No, but honestly," Carol would say, "I thought I was in love with Norman that time, but the first night we had him to dinner he buttered a whole piece of bread on the palm of his hand and I thought I'd die of mortification, so then I knew it wasn't love. I mean, love would be able to rise above a thing like that, wouldn't it?"

"You'd think so. Except perhaps it's a question of what something like that means. No manners. I'm not sure I could love someone who didn't have any manners."

"Maybe he just hadn't been taught. You can't blame someone for their upbringing. *Or* their parents. I mean, look at mine."

Betty would not be drawn into a discussion of Carol's parents, her mother and her assortment of fathers, one real and a succession of steps. "Maybe you wouldn't *blame* them. But, after all, Norman was sixteen or so when you went with him. By that time he should have noticed what people did with bread even if they hadn't taught him at home. You have to look around and see what's going on in the world. How could you love someone who wouldn't even take the trouble to look?"

"I couldn't love Norman, that's for sure. Or Brad. I sort of thought for a while . . . but he was always having to be reassured. I get very weary of boys who need to be reassured. I begin to think that probably there *is* something wrong with them, or why would I have to keep telling them there wasn't? No, not Brad."

"Or Weldon. Remember Weldon? He had an awfully sweet way about him. One of the things I liked best was that he used to hold my hand so nicely, as if he wouldn't jump six feet away if my mother walked in the room. That was nice."

"Yes, Weldon was nice," Carol said kindly, and kindly they consigned him to the impossibles.

"*Or* Matthew," Betty would say dreamily, wondering whether she'd have time to do her Latin in Study Hall tomorrow.

"Or John or Jake or Jim or Jeff or Joe," Carol had said, just a week or two ago, laughing as if she'd thought of something marvelously happy. "You see, we have it all ahead of us. I suppose," she added, "we'll have to know heartbreak."

"I should think so," Betty said amiably. "That's part of life, isn't it?"

Yes, surely there would be a measure of heartbreak in the cup of life, a cup they were prepared to quaff without a breath, if only it would get handed to them.

"After all," Betty had said, on more than one occasion, "we can hardly be said to have lived yet. Childhood, which we've gotten behind us, and all this irksome adolescence business, is just preliminary. I wish I were twenty."

"If I'm not living by the time I'm eighteen," Carol had said firmly, "I'll resign."

With its dimmers on, rear fender rattling, the truck came dashing down the road, and Betty lifted her head, forgetting Carol and the cup of life, Chicago and everything that had led her to this moment, because this moment seemed to her to be what everything else had been leading to. But no . . . not this moment itself. Surely something more was intended for her and the boy in the truck, or why would she have fallen so instantly in love? It wasn't her way, to fall in love. To like people, to get mildly exhilarated, to want to see some special person very specially, but not to fall in love with a young man she'd met once, who might wave to her as he went by in his truck, but then again might not. Who certainly never had her in his thoughts, as she had him.

The lights went out on the truck, the red shirt disappeared into the house, the sky darkened in a peculiar purplish mottling, like a curtain of blackberries.

What everything has been leading to, Betty thought, is this *consciousness* of Clifton Banks. Would Carol understand if I told her that I like the dishwasher not because it washes the dishes but because it somehow seems his?

No, she didn't think Carol would understand that, unless she'd fallen in love herself this week. Yet it was true. That machine which had been handled and soothed into obedience by Clifton Banks was dear to her as an extension, in some way, of him. All week she'd willingly done the chore over which she and her mother had wrangled for years, and her mother assigned her willingness to automation.

Would Carol think her touched if she confessed to having aligned everything neatly in her bureau, in her closet, because she wished to seem in her own mind an uncluttered, serene person, waiting in an ordered, graceful fashion for her love? She crumpled the letter she'd begun, and started over. "Dear Carol: Nothing much to report, really. The house is *darling*. My room here looks over a meadow, and there's a horse . . ."

3

IN CHICAGO SHE'D HAD SO many friends that her father had once threatened to rip the phone out of the wall.

"I mean it," he'd said, in an irritation frightening because it was so unlike him. "If that thing rings once more tonight, I'll tear it out of the wall and we'll never replace it, is that clear?"

"I'm sorry, Daddy," Betty had said nervously. "It was only Christine. She wanted to tell me about her new dress."

"Christine and her new dress or Marmaduke and his new space ship, I don't care. Just tell them they can't keep this phone running like a fever every night. You see them in the day, don't you? Why can't they get this information across then?"

"I don't know. We just . . . sort of like to telephone.

boy?"

"I don't know. It's all too long ago, and my nerves are too shot from the jangling of that bell to remember what I'm supposed to do tomorrow morning. How can I remember what I did when I was a boy? Yes, I suppose I did. But this is all out of proportion, Betty. Can't you see that yourself?"

In a way, she had seen. But to telephone a person you'd already talked to that day was as natural as breathing and to have a conversation lasting less than half an hour as unnatural as . . . as not telephoning at all. You lay back on the sofa, with your feet on its arm because it was good for the complexion to have your head lower than your feet, and you drawled over personalities, idiosyncrasies, plots and plans and wardrobes, and you were not aware of time passing until your father began to stir and mumble, or your mother made a remark that penetrated the almost total absorption of listening to Christine report what Alec had said to Gertrude in Study Hall. "Well, I'd better go now," you'd say, aware of impending strictures, and perhaps ten minutes later you actually hung up.

Yes, in a way she could see what her father meant. But the telephone calls had not lessened appreciably, nor had the phone been ripped out of the wall. It was simply that a sort of tension about its presence had arisen, flaring at times, abating at others. Betty decided (and tried) to shorten her conversations, but she really felt that reason was on her side.

"Well, anyway," she said to her mother now as they got ready to go into town and do the marketing, "that's one problem we don't have any more."

"What is?"

"The telephone. I don't call anybody, nobody calls me. It's too bad Daddy isn't around to hear how it doesn't ring."

"Darling, I'd sympathize with you, I truly would, except that in another couple of weeks school will start, and I imagine the phone will start at just about the same time, so let's enjoy this uncommon silence while we can."

28

"I don't see how anyone can enjoy silence. Besides, how can you be so sure that anyone will phone me? Maybe I'll be pariah. It isn't easy, starting in a new school in your last year of high."

"It wouldn't be for most people," Mrs. Wilder agreed. Her assurance that Betty would have no trouble was so complete that she didn't trouble to voice it.

Betty didn't know why this should annoy her faintly, but it did. She did not feel particularly apprehensive about the new school, and certainly it was nice to have parents whose confidence in you was so serene and utter. Still, it irked her not to elicit sympathy she did not need. Sympathy, she decided, should be like flowers —offered once in a while just for the offering. She smiled to herself, because the subject of flowers in their house had become almost—not quite—funny. Her mother had been telling her father for years how nice it was that some people brought other people flowers, and her father simply never took it personally, and never brought home a bunch of flowers.

It's sort of the same thing, she told herself now. Mother is so sure I'll be popular that she doesn't see any reason to reassure me, and Daddy is so fond of Mother that he doesn't see any reason for flowers to prove it. Ours is a family without gestures, and in a way it's a pity.

As they drove into town in the second-hand second car (Mr. Wilder used the better, first car for his work) she studied her mother from the corners of her eyes. An attractive woman. When she got dressed up and took a little time to use makeup, she could be extremely pretty. Does she ever, her daughter wondered, think that things might have been different? Wish that they might have been? To be that pretty and intelligent and spend your life in such a daily way, with practically no chance now of its ever being changed, heightened, made richer, seemed to Betty as chilling as a slow death. I'd die, she thought, I really would, to find myself practically forty and doomed to dailiness, with nothing but dailiness to look back on. She hoped, gently and compassionately, that her mother never longed for heights

29

or depths, and in a burst of tenderness offered to get dinner that night.

"When we get home," she said, "you take a bath and get into a negligee and just sit. Have a glass of sherry or something, and sit in the living room, and I'll serve you on a tray." It was a poor substitute for colorful living, but the best that she could offer. It was a gesture.

Like many gestures, it fell somewhere between the giver and the receiver. Mrs. Wilder was touched, but she was also preoccupied. In her mind was a cornucopia from which spilled jars and frozen-food packages which she could label—as sidewalk artists did, she'd heard, in London—*all my own work*. She saw jellies glowing like ruby corundums, topazes, minty emeralds. She saw pale curries, brown stews, divers spicy and daftly shaped canapés created, boxed, endorsed and frozen by her own hands. She was exhilarated and confused by half a dozen cookbooks, a hundred plans, and no experience. There was no place in this vision for a negligee (which she didn't own anyway) and dinner on a tray.

"That's lovely of you, dear," she said. "And I'll take you up on the dinner offer. You can cook something simple for us while I prepare the meat and vegetables for the Danish Stew."

"Danish Stew?"

"I thought we could freeze tonight," Mrs. Wilder said happily. "And I've found the most marvelous recipe for something called Danish Stew. It has cardamon in it."

Just as I said, Betty told herself in a nettled way. A family without gestures. They not only aren't made, they aren't even recognized. Danish Stew. "I think it's silly to go to all that trouble when you can buy stuff so easily. It's practically ingratitude to science, you know. Science labors for years and comes up with the flash-frozen trout, and then women turn their backs and go back to the mortar and pestle."

"I don't intend to flash-freeze trout. I expect it isn't done with a mortar and pestle, anyway."

"I'm talking principles. To my way of thinking, it's as archaic to put up watermelon pickle or Danish Stew as it would be to leave penicillin out of the picture if you had a disease. I mean, what's science for?"

"The only creative aspect of housekeeping is cooking," Mrs. Wilder said imperturbably. "I've never had a real chance to try it. Not on such a scale. A freezer *and* shelves in the basement—it's just too good to be true. And since your idea of a day in the kitchen is to make a pan of instant fudge, I don't think I can accept you as an equal in this argument."

"But you'll accept me as equal in the cooking part. And that's where principle comes in. Since I have all this faith in science, I think it's a betrayal of self for me to help you make frozen stew."

"If it's the most drastic way in which you're ever untrue to yourself, you'll be fortunate. Really, Betty. I'm tired of arguing about it, and as far as I'm concerned, if you do even part of your share of the housework, you can leave the freezing and jarring—or whatever they call what you do to jellies—to me. Maybe if I'm not too weary," she continued in an altered, thoughtful tone, "I'll do some jelly tonight, too."

I'd be too weary if I were you, Betty thought, but decided she'd said enough.

They drove into Norwood in silence. A neat town, with a good-sized square, a clapboard church at one end and the town hall with jail at the other, and two long, wide main streets crossing each other to comprise the main shopping area. Norwood, N. Y., population 24,000 and growing.

"Do you think we'll live here long?" Betty asked.

"I imagine so. This is the best territory that they've given your father. I mean, the best territory there is," she said proudly. "I don't see anywhere to go from here."

Betty shuddered a little at the implication of the remark, but her mother drove competently, smoothly along, pulled into a supermarket parking lot, stopped the car and said, with no evidence of anything but pleasure in the task ahead, "Come along, dear. This is going to take ages."

Betty wanted to feel sorry for her mother, who took

such touching pleasure in the homely job of marketing. Except, she realized—not for the first time—it's difficult to feel sorry for people who don't feel sorry for themselves. You can think they're misguided, that they've missed the entire point of life, that you wouldn't be in their shoes for any offer. But you can't pity them.

With a sigh she transferred the pity to herself and followed her mother resignedly into the supermarket, where there was music playing, and a flower stall scenting the air, and aisle upon aisle of food—both in its natural state and miraculously meddled with by science. Hands on a metal shopping cart, Mrs. Wilder stood a moment surveying this bright kingdom.

"Do you ever think how we take for granted things that queens with all their money could never have commanded?" She swept a hand through air. "Think what Marie Antoinette would have said to this."

"She wouldn't have been doing the shopping."

Mrs. Wilder laughed. "All right. What she would have said to gas heat and indoor plumbing, then? All her diamond necklaces could never have bought those."

Betty admitted that probably the poor queen would happily have traded a tiara or two for just one warm room at Versailles, and would undoubtedly have been wonder-struck at the sight of a modern bathroom.

"When I was young," she said, and did not see, because she was looking at the flowers, her mother's quick amused glance, "I used to think, sort of proudly, you know, how people in olden times would be so amazed at the things we've managed to bring about. A Connecticut Yankee attitude, I suppose. But now I think more about what people are going to have when we're dead and gone, except I suppose nothing would amaze us, would it?"

"Because everything keeps getting predicted."

"I'll bet one day they'll fix it so people don't get old. I mean, I expect we'll go on *getting* old, but it won't show."

"That would be nice," Mrs. Wilder sighed.

"Why, Mother, I didn't mean you."

"I know you didn't, dear. Well, let's get on with the

32

marketing. We have to go to the hardware store after this, because I've decided to be a gardener, and I'll need tools. And then on the way home we'll stop at Mrs. Banks's stand for fruit and vegetables."

"Oh?" said Betty, catching her breath slightly at the name, at the prospect that Clifton Banks might possibly be at the stand. "We can get them here," she pointed out, masking her interest, but knowing quite well what her mother would say.

"When you see the stuff Mrs. Banks has, you'll understand."

Betty was strongly tempted to go on making conversation about Mrs. Banks, in hope that it would lead to the son, just because she'd like so much to talk about him. On the other hand, she didn't want her mother to know that she wanted to talk about him.

So far, Mrs. Wilder had apparently not noticed anything different in Betty's demeanor, but apparently wasn't always an operative word in her mother's case. She had a way of detecting Betty's moods—and not saying anything about it—that her daughter did not welcome. It isn't, she told herself, that I want to be secretive, it's more that I want, and need, privacy. Mother gets too *aware* of me. Even when she pretends not to, I can feel her knowing things I'd rather have for myself.

Carol had often complained that her mother was obtuse. "Honestly, I think I could be on the verge of suicide before Mother even got around to noticing me. I suppose if I shoved my head in the oven she might ask if I had something on my mind." Betty had said, and thought, that that was a darned shame. But sometimes she wondered which was worse. A mother who was so perceptive that without meaning to she took away your sense of having anything to yourself, or one who never understood at all that there were times when you had to share. Carol, of course, could share with her friends, and on the whole that was probably preferable.

"Come on," she said to her mother, and to the strains of the "Blue Danube" they set off.

The supermarket was air-conditioned, and when they came out laden nearly an hour later, heat that had not seemed too intense when they drove in now seemed to Betty just about insupportable.

"My gosh," she said, stowing the last of the bags in the back seat, "everything's going to be melted, including me."

Mrs. Wilder hesitated. "I suppose we really ought to go home and get this stuff put away, and then go to Mrs. Banks's stand. Only I did want to get a few things in the hardware store." Betty groaned, and Mrs. Wilder looked impatient. "You haven't been overworked."

"Not yet. We've got the rest of the day ahead of us."

"Betty, there are times when I could scream at your attitude."

"I know," said Betty contritely. "I'm awful."

"Well, you are. And don't think you can get around me merely by saying it."

But the fact is, Mrs. Wilder thought, she *can* get around me merely by saying such things, and she always has been able to. Around me, and around her father. Do we spoil her, she wondered, or just love her? In these days of Psychology for the Millions, of inescapable (and contradictory) Advice to Parents, it was difficult to tell.

The hardware store was directly across the street, and there was a drugstore beside it. "Let's leave the car here," Mrs. Wilder said, "and while I get a few gardening tools, you can go in that drugstore and have a Coke, if you're so hot."

"You're sure you don't mind?" Betty asked as they crossed the street. She was, now that it was mentioned, dying for a Coke. "I could help you and then we could both have one."

"No, no. I don't want one. I want a trowel, and a hoe, and a few other things, and I want to discuss them with the man, and we have to get some of those groceries home to the refrigerator. So you have your Coke and come in for me. Don't be too long."

The small drugstore was dim, cool, empty save for the chemist, the soda-fountain girl, and a young boy making a careful study of the comics. Betty walked to the fountain, sat on a stool, and looked at herself in the mirror. She always looked at herself in store mirrors

34

and shopwindows, sometimes covertly, sometimes, as now, quite frankly—since the chemist was occupied with his trade behind a glass partition, the girl was washing glasses, and nothing short of the entrance of Gabriel, or possibly a big-league ballplayer, could have lured that boy out of his present investigations. Betty knew, because George, for all his scientific mind, had also been a comic enthusiast. She'd told him once that it was a little discouraging to play third fiddle to bugs and Pogo, but all he'd replied was, "Insects. I have no traffic with bugs," and returned his attention to Pogo.

As always—nearly always—her reflection pleased her. She had a nice figure, rich brown hair, a fine short nose, eyes she could usually consider green. In her lime-colored cotton dress, only slightly rumpled, she decided she looked what she was always wanting to look . . . serene, untroubled by outside factors, such as heat.

It seemed to Betty that there were two things above all desirable in a woman. One was to seem ever tranquil, coolly poised. The other was to be known as a person who said the right thing. Betty Wilder never fumbles, she always seems to know the right thing to say. That's the way she would like people to speak of her. But though she made a point of never complaining about the heat (one way of seeming cool), in her most self-satisfied moments she could not think of herself as a person who was poised and always said the right thing. Too many recollections immediately rose to confront her. She'd remember the times when, eager not to miss the point, she laughed before the joke was finished. Times when, in order to prove the quickness of her mind, she made a glib answer when a thought-out answer was called for. Times when she didn't know what to say and stood silence-struck when the right word was absolutely necessary.

Oh, well, she thought now, no doubt that comes with the maturity Carol is always piping for. When maturity rears its peculiar head, then the right word will be easily said. The jingly sense of this pleased her, and she said it to herself a couple of times. Then she coughed to get the attention of the soda-fountain girl, dreamily washing glasses.

"A Coke, please."

"Oh, sure. Large or small?"

"Have the large," said a voice, once heard and completely remembered.

She looked up to find Clifton Banks beside her. She had not heard him come in, but here he was, so close that she could see more clearly what she had noticed in the kitchen that afternoon—the innocent and too old look of his young face. The sickle lines from nose to mouth were deep, and he had newsboy eyes—limpid, determined, hopeful.

Betty tried to show in her own eyes nothing but casual greeting. The radiance she felt, the bell-like joy, would send a man who didn't expect it flying. This, she reminded herself, is no high-school boy to be flattered around. This is a man, a young one but with a man's work and a man's way to make. Far beyond eyelash-batting, Clifton Banks.

So she looked at him with what objectivity she could, and said, "That's lovely of you. A small one would really do."

He sat down beside her. "Oh, have the large," he said. "I'm a heavy spender."

This delighted her. She had a feeling that probably everything about him was going to delight her, and immediately became preoccupied with the question, would anything about her delight him? Was he too busy to be reachable? Or already delighted by someone else, so that—in the fashion of lovers—he'd have eyes but see not, ears but hear not, except when the one person was present? How can I charm you? she asked him silently. What sort of girl do you like?

The girl put two large Cokes before them, and said, "How's your mother, Cliff?"

"Working too hard."

"Normal, then."

Is this the girl? Betty wondered. She's sort of gorgeous, and probably nice. Is this the one he sees to the exclusion of all others?

"Have you two met?" Clifton asked. The two girls shook their heads. "Well, this is Beatrice Roman. Uh—"

he looked at Betty "—sorry, I remember the Wilder part, but—"

"Betty," she said in a downcast way, caught Beatrice's knowing eyes, and gave a small self-conscious smile.

"Betty," he said. "Betty Wilder. She'll be going to school here," he explained to Beatrice. "She and her folks just came from Chicago." He turned to Betty. "Beatrice is going into her last year high. How about you?"

"Me too," Betty said to this grown-up who was arranging for the new child to meet a little friend.

"Good," said the grown-up. "Maybe you can get together."

Beatrice now looked definitely amused. "Be glad to," she said, "if I ever get out of the soda-pop mines."

Her voice, dry and pleasant, caught Betty's interest. Strange-looking girl, but definitely attractive. Black hair wound in braids around her head in a fashion few girls could get away with, an oval face, a smile that was utterly friendly, and gray eyes that had in them some bright flippancy that made you wonder about the smile.

"Maybe Sunday," said Clifton, pursuing his *in loco parentis* role.

Is he a good-deeder? Betty wondered with dismay. The lawn, the dishwasher, and now this? Oh, surely not. Good-deeders, poor things, were such bores. Don't be a bigot, she told herself irritably. A person can be kind and thoughtful without being labeled a good-deeder. Anyway, there are two sure ways to know a good-deeder. One, they are scared to death you won't notice what they've done, and, two, you positively hate thanking them. Clifton answered to neither of these charges. He'd done their lawn and dishwasher almost in passing, almost as if he didn't notice himself—in the press of an occupied day—that he had done them, and she found herself now quite willing to thank him for his intervention in her behalf. It was a bit scary, thinking of the first day in a new school, and this Beatrice was (you didn't need to know her a minute to see it) someone to be reckoned with. Someone to be reckoned with was good to know on your first day of school.

37

"Sure," said Beatrice. "I'll look you up."

There was no way, of course, to tell whether she really meant it. Two customers came in just then, and Beatrice left to take their orders.

"What are you doing in town?" Clifton asked. "Just looking around?"

"Mother never just looks around. We're shopping." At his smile, she added defensively, "I got hot, so Mother gave me a few minutes off."

At this, Clifton looked a bit hurried. "Are you busy tonight?" he asked in a curious, almost reluctant tone.

She overlooked the tone, heard the words, and, transported with joy, wanted to leap into the silence with, No, oh, no, I'm not, ask what you want to ask, Clifton, Cliff. But she stayed her tongue the necessary first moment, and then stayed it while she thought. She had told her mother she'd help with this project tonight. That she herself thought it was silly and unnecessary did not alter the fact that her mother was eager and happy and would love to have someone to share the beginning of her cooking adventure with. She probably won't ask me to do it often, Betty told herself. I'd be awful, even if I could get away with it, and I probably could, to walk out on her tonight. There were some things you just didn't do.

She drew a regretful, silent breath and said, "Yes, I am busy, I have to help launch my mother on her new career."

"New career?" He sounded less disappointed than approving.

"She's going to can and freeze and bottle everything she can lay her hands on, apparently. Mother has always been a frustrated cook, and now she has the room and the equipment to get herself unfrustrated. I promised to help her."

She was piqued but not surprised when his approbation increased. I'll bet he doesn't know what the word lazy means. Or even leisurely, for that matter. Why did I have to fall in love with someone like that? George, diligent enough about his hobby, still understood an indolent medium better than he understood any other. Catch George approving if you said you couldn't make a date because you had to help your mother. "Help her do what?" he says and then, "Your mother?" As if neither help nor mother was a word he'd ever encountered. Certainly, when with any degree of grace he could, he avoided both. George, of course, was a child compared with Clifton.

And now Clifton, with exasperating alacrity, said, "Sure, I can see where you'd want to help."

Can you? thought Betty, and waited. But he sipped his Coke and was apparently not going to pursue the matter. Should I tell him that there are three hundred and sixty-four other evenings in the year, and so far I haven't promised one of them? No, better not. With some boys she'd have done it easily, but Clifton awed her too much. Oh, well, she thought cheerfully, he did ask. On the heels of that thought came another. Was it—oh, misery—possible that he would not ask again at all? He'd made a gesture and been refused, and now he might consider that to be that. He even, now that she thought it over, seemed a little relieved.

It was, as Carol frequently complained, a man's world. And in this man's world, Betty thought now, a girl has to take what she can get by wiles, subtlety, coercion, or blandishment. But she can never, not ever, say simply, honestly, and aloud, This is what I'd like. All this week I've pined and wondered, hoped and hardly dared to hope, that maybe this Clifton, this man of all men, would notice me, would turn his gaze my way one day and find me pleasing. And lo, he's not only looked, he's tossed me a crumb. So I scream *nectar* and devour it and look around for more. But are there to be any more? How do I know? How in this man's world would I know?

Quite resentful, but unable to show that either, she sipped an unnectarish Coke and noticed that the continuing silence did not seem in the least to trouble Clifton. He finished his drink, smiled at her amiably, got to his feet and felt in his dungaree pockets for change. "Here you are, Bea."

"Right. So long, Cliff."

"See you," he said, and then to Betty, "You too, I hope."

39

"Thank you for the Coke," she said. A bit tartly? She didn't care.

"Pleasure."

He was gone.

Beatrice Roman came back and said quizzically, "You must be a miracle-worker. I've never known Cliff to come right out and ask someone for a date like that."

You know him so well? Betty wondered, instantly jealous. But Beatrice seemed interested, not distressed. Then she was not the girl? Or was she simply very wise? Oh, well, what difference does it make to me? I am going to forget him. A week is quite enough to allot to a hopeless love. Besides, no one can fall in love in a week. I was carried away by his good looks, his newsboy eyes, his kindness, his . . .

She had to say something, and she did not want to talk about Clifton Banks. "I should think it would be fun working here," she offered lamely. "Do you just do it summers?"

If Beatrice resented the change of subject, she didn't show it. "Gosh, no. I wish it was so. I work here after school, and Saturdays. Sunday he doesn't open, or Sunday I'd be working, too. Wouldn't I, Boss?" she said as the pharmacist came out from behind his glass wall to put a package at the end of the counter. He was a slender, pallid man, somewhere between thirty and sixty, Betty thought.

"Wouldn't you what?" he said.

"Wouldn't I be working here Sundays if you were open Sundays?"

"I hope so," he said earnestly. His voice was as pale as his complexion. "Where's Jack? This stuff for Mrs. Eckles has to go right out."

Beatrice looked at the clock. "He'll be here any second, Boss. I'll send him right out. This is Betty Wilder. Her family just moved to town. This is my boss, Mr. Perkins, Betty."

"How do you do?" said Mr. Perkins, looking at the ceiling. He went back behind his wall.

"Not talky," Beatrice explained. "But a nice guy. I always call him the Boss. To build up his ego, you know."

"He looks as if he might need it."

"Who doesn't?" said Beatrice philosophically. "But the Boss more than most. I've seen more color in an empty bottle, but of course, that isn't his fault, so I call him the Boss in case it gives him a lift. Not that you'd ever know. From looking at him, I mean. *Jack*, it's about time. . . ."

A boy of about thirteen, oddly familiar-looking, came in without undue haste. "Betty, this is my brother, Jack. This is Betty Wilder. She's new in town."

"Hi," said Jack. He nodded toward the end of the counter. "That all?"

"Yes. To Mrs. Eckles. Pronto."

Jack picked up the package, grunted something at the comic-reading boy, who grunted back without looking up, and went out with a wave of his hand.

"You come right back," Beatrice called after him. "And keep your eyes on where you're going."

Mrs. Wilder came in as Jack went out, saw the two girls talking, and smiled. Betty introduced her and asked if she'd like something, but Mrs. Wilder said her hardware shopping had taken longer than she'd expected.

"It always does, of course," she said. "There's something about hardware stores."

"Isn't there, though?" said Beatrice. "I get that way in hat departments, myself."

"Hats?" said Mrs. Wilder. "I didn't think there was a girl left in America who bought hats."

"Oh, I don't buy them," Beatrice said. "But how I love to look at them. Well, been nice meeting you," she said to the two Wilders as a group of young people came in.

"Get ready to slave, Bea," said one of the boys. "We all want something fancy."

"And we all want something different," a girl added.

They crowded up to the counter, talking and laughing. Betty, conscious that these were people she might know soon but definitely did not know now, urged her mother out of the store.

"Come on, Mom. The groceries will be getting too much sun."

"I must say," Mrs. Wilder exclaimed, stopping in her

tracks, her voice perfectly audible, "it's a fine time for you to start worrying about the groceries. After all—"

"Mom, let's go," Betty said fiercely, looking straight into her mother's eyes and commanding her to shut up.

Mrs. Wilder got the message and went without further protest. But she was stiffly silent as they started home.

Oh, really! Betty thought. Parents are impossible. Here I give up a date and everything for her, and now look. She wasn't sure what she meant by and everything, but she knew what she meant by impossible. This was not the only time her mother had shown this sudden obtuseness, this lack of sensitivity to Betty's feelings about her contemporaries. Had *her* mother ever stopped in front of a field of strangers to berate her? For that matter, had her mother's mother ever laughed or talked too loudly when visiting her daughter's school? Well, her daughter has, Betty continued wildly, lost in a forest of pronouns. It was not to be believed that a woman as fine-grained as her mother was in most ways could say "my Betty" or even "my little girl" in public. But she'd been known to do it. Not two hours ago, Betty reminded herself bitterly, I was saying how perceptive she was—

Mrs. Wilder thought, What did I do this time? What? Something in the drugstore, but what? I met her friend —Beatrice, is it?—such an appealing child. Did Betty want me to remain, to talk with them? No, that would not be it. Well, what? That I made a perfectly justified remark about her sudden hurry? We left the groceries sitting in the car for almost half an hour, and all of a sudden they might have been melting ice cubes, the way she was anxious to get to them. As neither she nor Betty knew anyone else in the drugstore, Mrs. Wilder never gave the entering group a thought. Nor thought —since, in any case, she hadn't been shouting—that she should have lowered her voice and hastened out on their approach.

Baffled and put out, she drove without a word.

Mrs. Wilder, who had a very good memory, tended to think of her whole life as something tangible, something she could look at whenever she wanted to. Her life, she felt, was like a box with a lot of compartments. She carried this box around with her, and at a moment's notice could open any compartment and examine the part where she was ten, sixteen, thirty. Year by year, as Betty grew, her mother would open the appropriate compartment and give long study to what lay within. Seventeen, she thought now. Often enough in the past months she'd pondered over the compartment labeled seventeen. What about my mother would send me into despondency when I was seventeen? Well, the same thing that made me despondent when I was seven, and twelve, and twenty. She simply didn't pay much attention to me. Loved me, no doubt, but simply couldn't, or wouldn't, show it. I'm not like that with Betty. I love her, and show my love. My mother and I were never friends in a real sense, but Betty and I are. Most of the time. And I'm reasonable. I don't expect my daughter's friendship at all times. Young people have other things on their minds than filial relationships. I take that into account and don't brood when she's thoughtless, and don't—really don't—get hurt. I expect a certain amount of thoughtlessness, and remember well that I certainly displayed it.

Oh, well, she decided, whatever it was, it's over. No use prolonging this silence. "Your friend's name is Beatrice?" she said. "She's very pretty."

"Isn't she?" Betty couldn't decide whether to mention Clifton Banks, decided not to, and said, "She's going into her last year high, too."

Mr. Wilder often said of them that either they had the best dispositions in the world, or the poorest attention spans, because neither could ever stay angry.

4

ON SUNDAY MORNING THE phone rang, and Mrs. Wilder, who was closest, picked it up. "For you," she said, handing it to Betty. "I told you it would start happening."

It won't be Cliff, Betty thought. There's no point hoping, because it won't be. And it wasn't, so she was right.

"Betty? This is Beatrice Roman. I wondered if maybe you'd like to come over to my house. I mean, if you aren't doing something else."

"Just a second, Beatrice." Betty looked at her mother, who was looking meditatively toward the kitchen. "Mom, this is Beatrice Roman, and she wants me to visit her for a while, okay?"

"Of course, dear."

"Beatrice? Mother says fine. Only how do I get there?"

"I'll have Cliff Banks pick you up," Beatrice said easily. "He's coming over here anyway, to pick up my brother Gil. They're going out on a job together. I warn you, this place is a madhouse—"

Even over the phone there was evidence of that. Some opera was blaring in the background, and in the foreground a child was screaming, "Bea, Bea, Bea, Bea . . ." Betty couldn't tell if it was a boy's voice or a girl's, but it kept up that steady Bea, Bea, Bea, all the time they talked, and once a male voice called, "Beatrice, get off the phone!"

"I practically just got on," Beatrice said loudly, without rancor. "See what I mean?" she said to Betty. "A madhouse. If you want to risk it."

"Happy to." She added in an offhand tone, "You said Cliff Banks would pick me up?"

"I'll give him a ring and tell him. All *right*, Gil . . . I'm *getting* off. Gotta go, Betty. You can see what I mean . . . a madhouse."

"Well, now, that was nice of her," Mrs. Wilder said. "And Clifton Banks is going to pick you up?"

"He has to go over there anyway. He's going to do some sort of job with Beatrice's brother."

"On Sunday, too?" Mrs. Wilder murmured. "Doesn't that boy ever give himself a rest?"

"You're going to make that plum jelly, I bet. And it's Sunday for you, too."

"But I'm having fun. It isn't the same thing at all."

Maybe it is, Betty thought, going up to her room. Maybe he's the sort of person who wants to work all the time and just adores every second of it. Somehow, it was still to be hoped that he worked because he had to. A person would have to be terribly rigid not to want to rest, to be indolent, to be spendthrift, now and then, of time.

Her attention wandered from that to the question of Clifton's relationship with Beatrice Roman. Was Beatrice's ease of manner concerning him the result of a long acquaintance or a very close one, or both? A girl that striking and self-assured would be very hard to get off a man's mind. Even if you could, there was the matter of loyalty. Beatrice had shown herself willing to be friends, and the willingness in a way constituted a friendship already begun. Betty had strict notions about friendship, and one was that you did not attempt to win away the boy friend of a girl friend. It simply wasn't done.

She saw herself, in the months to come, friendly with both of them, in love with Cliff, obliged to conceal it, to watch their love as if indifferently, or, even worse, as if happily, and the picture was too awful. And it was no use telling herself that she was not in love with Cliff, because she was. She could not get him out of her thoughts for a moment. *I wish I hadn't said I'd go. I wish I hadn't gone into that drugstore, and so had never met her.*

But he did ask me if I was busy that night. Nobody ever says are you busy without intending a date. He could have been doing it on purpose. They might have had a quarrel and he asked me to make her jealous. *Oh, nonsense. A person like Clifton Banks didn't stoop to such levels. No?* she asked herself wryly. *Who in love doesn't stoop to any level, if at that level he hopes to find help? I've never been in love before, but I've had a glimpse now and then, and definitely in those glimpses I saw that there are times when love has to stoop. Remember how poor Carol would abandon all pride (and she was a proud girl) to phone Brad if he did not phone her? The fact that she got tired of him eventually has nothing to do with it. While she was in love, Carol was helpless not to stoop. We're all helpless in love.*

Betty sat down with her wayward thoughts, waiting for Clifton Banks to come, thinking that, anyway, today she would know. She would find out if he and Beatrice were in love with each other.

She started a little at her mother's voice calling from downstairs. "Betty? Betty, don't you think you could help me a little before your friend comes for you?"

Betty descended to the kitchen in a martyred state. It was one thing to decide, because it was a new house, a new life, because—more to the point—you'd seen that

Clifton Banks liked that sort of thing, to help your mother with the housework, and help her in a good, generous-minded way. It was another to be pursued this way, evenings, Sundays, all the time.

She put on an apron and said, without hope, "I don't see that I can get much done."

"You can begin pitting the plums, that will be a big help. When is he coming for you?"

"I don't know."

"Then how do you know you can't get much done?"

There was no answer to that. Betty picked up a paring knife and began to halve the purple, silver-hazed Damson plums. There was a great bag of them, and as she dropped the pitted halves in a large wooden bowl a sharp sweet odor rose in the kitchen. Mrs. Wilder hummed as she measured sugar and water. The late summer air, hot and zinnia-flavored, drifted through open windows and the open back door.

Betty thought, relenting, that this was rather nice. Even if Clifton had not been calling for her to take her to Beatrice's. Even if, as she might so easily have been, she'd been going to spend the entire afternoon here in the kitchen with her mother and the plums and the thick boiling syrup, it would really have been nice. But she wasn't going to commit herself by saying so, and she listened eagerly, even as she and her mother exchanged desultory comments, for the sound of the truck in the driveway.

That truck, she thought. I am actually going to ride in that truck. A shiver of elation went through her, and, without meaning to, she laughed.

"What's funny?" said her mother with a happy smile.

"I don't know, Mother. Nothing. I just feel good, I guess." Because certainly she could not say, I am delirious with joy because I'm going to ride in Clifton Banks's pickup truck. I've mooned over that truck for ages, like the goosegirl staring at the castle on the hill, and now, now, now, I'm going to ride in it. "I just feel good," she repeated, and her mother worked on with a happy expression.

So, by good chance, that was how Clifton Banks, coming up the back-porch steps, found them, working and laughing together. Oh, joy, thought Betty. It couldn't have been better if I'd planned it. When had she ever before cared so desperately what a boy thought of her, wanted so much to appear to be what he wanted a girl to be? Never. Never had she altered, or considered altering, her own way of being so as to fit a boy's fancy. They liked her as she was, or she never even knew they hadn't.

But, for love—one day she must tell Carol that for love you were willing to change anything, everything. For love, you said, However you want me, that way will I be. Carol, for all her loving Brad and Norman, and I, though I almost loved George, did not know this.

"Come in, come in," said Mrs. Wilder cheerfully. "How are you, Clifton? I may call you Clifton, mayn't I?"

"I want you to," he said. To Betty his voice was as rich and warm as the summer air itself, his eyes, when he looked at her, azure as the summer sky. "I have a commission to pick you up," he said.

"I know. I hope it doesn't take you out of your way."

It didn't, and she knew it didn't—he went right past the house, after all—but she had to say something non-committal, or he and her mother would both guess what she was feeling.

"Not at all," he said. "Everything all right here?" He walked over and peered into the dishwasher. "No more trouble with this? Shouldn't be—it's a good machine."

In a minute, Betty thought, he'll get out a stetho-scope. Yet there was something very winning in the professional way he looked at machines, in the clinical way he inquired after them.

He wore, despite Sunday, his usual dungarees and cotton flannel shirt, a uniform so becoming that it might have been designed for him.

"Will you have a cup of coffee?" Mrs. Wilder asked, since he seemed to be in no special hurry.

"That'd be fine." He sat down at the table with Betty. George would have remained standing until Mrs. Wilder seated herself. But George would never have smiled in that warm interested way, nor said that Mrs.

48

Wilder looked like someone who'd been making Damson plum jam all her life.

"Do I?" Mrs. Wilder said with pleasure. "I can't remember when I've had so much fun."

If this seemed a pathetic admission to Betty, it clearly did not to the other two. Clifton looked over the plums and observed that she had a good batch, and Mrs. Wilder explained that they'd been bought at his mother's stand.

"Where do you get the produce, Clifton?" she asked. "That is, I know you grow some, but surely not all?"

"No, not all. I go over to the market early in the morning. I'm a pretty good buyer now, if I do say so."

"You're remarkable," Mrs. Wilder murmured in a low voice.

Yes, thought Betty, remarkable. So among other things he also buys fruit and vegetables early in the morning. What time does he get up? When does he ever rest, or play, or just do nothing?

"Is that your horse out there?" she said suddenly.

Clifton nodded. "Calvin."

"Do you ride him?"

"Calvin's a work horse. I use him in the truck garden, and for hauling wood. But, yes, I ride him. He understands my limitations and I understand his. On that basis, we go out together from time to time."

"I'd be afraid to ride a horse."

"You wouldn't be afraid of Calvin. It's like riding a sofa." Clifton grinned, but he did not, Betty noticed, actually offer Calvin's services, and for fear he might feel he had to, or simply for fear he would, she changed the subject.

"It was awfully nice of Beatrice to invite me, wasn't it?"

He looked surprised. "No. I thought she would. Did you meet her?" he asked Mrs. Wilder.

"I met her briefly. She's lovely-looking."

"I've known her since we were kids," Clifton said absently. He glanced at Betty. "If it's okay with you, we'd better get along. Gil Roman and I have to work over at Moore's greenhouses today, and today's already got a good head start."

"What are you going to do there?" Mrs. Wilder asked curiously.

"Put up slathouses for boxwood slips."

"And are you always doing something? Always working?"

Clifton had a relaxed laugh, one he used easily. It came now, almost in place of a reply, but he added as he lifted his big muscular body from the chair, "Once in a while I take some time off. Go out and shoot at crows, or maybe fish."

Betty, watching her mother watch Cliff, thought, She likes him. She finds him admirable and good. An obscure vision touched her consciousness, a vision in which Clifton was a major part—in which Clifton was all. One in which he loved her, and, in the background, her parents nodded at them with pleasure, finding him good and admirable. For the first time in her life, and on so little acquaintance, Betty vaguely perceived why girls settled for home and husband.

But what, she thought suddenly, as if she were waking, am I thinking of? Like a dream, which can be sensed but not possibly remembered, this perception of the future passed from her mind, and she looked at Clifton a little coolly, as you regard someone who has threatened you in a dream. You know it is no doing of the person himself, you accept responsibility for your own dreams. And still, for a little while, you regard him suspiciously.

Clifton caught something of this. "Anything wrong?" he asked mildly.

"Oh, no," she said in confusion. She jumped to her feet. "Mother, I'm *sorry* to leave you with all this," she said falsely.

Undeceived but cooperative, Mrs. Wilder said she knew, she knew. "Perhaps there'll be something left to do when you get home, dear."

"You save something for me," Betty said, not to be outdone.

In the truck, Clifton said, "Your mother's awfully nice."

"Mmm," said Betty inattentively. She was savoring the old stale smell, looking with enraptured eyes at the dirty floorboard, the dusty instrument panel. This was the inside of his truck, and here was she where she'd dreamed of being, beside him, with him, and this time when the truck went dashing down past Bolt's Hollow to town she would not be left behind with longing heart and yearning eyes. She was with him. She released a great sigh of contentment and stared through the grimy windshield.

"What I like," Clifton was saying loudly, over the anguished rattling and roaring of the pickup in motion, "is the way you work together."

"You just like work, don't you?" she asked happily. She was hardly paying attention to what he said, so occupied was she with the sensation of being with him.

"I'm not that crazy about it. Not as much as you and your mother seem to think. Sometimes I think I keep at it just because I'm lazy."

"Lazy?"

"In a way. I get started doing something, and I'm too lazy to stop."

Betty laughed. "That's just silly." It was fun to say something like that to Clifton. Fun, and a little daring. It wouldn't have been daring with anyone else, but with Clifton it was.

"No," he said seriously. "It's always easier to keep doing something than to stop." She thought he might elaborate, but he didn't.

She fixed her guessing eyes on his profile, then looked at her own hands, lying in her lap, and realized that she didn't have to talk. He certainly was not like anybody else.

They were driving through deserted Sunday streets in the south end of Norwood. Shops were closed and empty-faced (except for a dingy candy store with a newspaper stand outside), sidewalks were littered and grayer-seeming than on weekdays, a few cars passed, and an occasional pedestrian, looking homeless. Clifton turned onto a street just off the shopping district, and slowed down. It was a drab block of brown clapboard or yellow imitation-brick houses, dispirited small lawns, windows with placards in them—*Hand Laundry and Sewing. Watch Hospital. Rooms.*

Betty's spirits felt a sudden touch of damp. "Is this where Beatrice lives?" she asked reluctantly.

"Just down the street."

Not liking herself, not wanting to feel it, unable not to feel it, Betty felt revulsion and an ardent desire to be back in her own trim clean house set in its pretty lawn. She had always been like this about streets like this, and had always tried to hide it. Tawdry places, poor bleak places, dismayed her and she wanted not to look at them, wanted not to know that they existed. There were streets in Chicago where she would never go, or, if she had to, went through with deliberately blank eyes, and quickly. There were certain streets, offices, homes, that fairly whimpered, I've given up, I'm a mess, I'm hopeless . . . pity me. But Betty could not pity these places. She only didn't like them. She only wanted nothing to do with them.

And now Beatrice lived on just such a mean street, in just such a house.

The school she'd gone to in Chicago was ill-proportioned and ugly in appearance, but she'd grown too accustomed to take offense. Besides, the school was inescapable.

This was not.

I want to go home, Betty said. She did not say it aloud, but the words were there. She turned to Clifton Banks. I'll tell him I've forgotten something, I'll say I'm suddenly not feeling well, I'll say something, anything, only away from this street I must go. . . .

"Here we are," said Clifton. He pulled on the emergency brake and jumped out of the truck before she could speak. Slowly, Betty opened the door on her side and got out. A big house, the Romans'. Yellow pretend brick. Window boxes of determined geraniums. A scooter lying on its side directly in her path, a fat biscuit-colored dog lying on his side just beyond it, several bikes parked on a lawn that was mostly dirt. She looked at Clifton's back without seeing it and followed him up the steps to the big porch. There were three grayish wicker rocking chairs on the porch, and a tricycle and a doll with an arm missing. There were panels of colored glass on each side of the front door, and when Clifton rang the bell it played a tune in the house.

What a prig I am, Betty thought, yearning for home.

"Betty! Cliff!" Beatrice flung the door open, greeted them like returned travelers, drew them into a large hall in which there was a piano, an aspidistra in a brown bowl, a round rag rug, and a mission table piled with magazines, caps, little toy cars, and sheet music. There was an odor of cooking that at home would have been delicious but here was merely overwhelming, thick.

"Hi, Bea," said Cliff, in his nice warm voice.

"Hello," said the prig, with no tone at all in hers.

"This is lovely," said Beatrice, apparently meaning it. "Come along and meet Mama, Betty. She's heard all about you."

Heard all what about me? Betty wondered stiffly. How could she have heard anything, since you don't know anything yourself? What do you mean, heard all about me? And then she thought, I'm not very fond of myself right now. It didn't put her in a better mood.

The kitchen was enormous. It had a big round table covered with yellow oilcloth that was cracked at the corners. It had the biggest refrigerator Betty had ever seen. It had both an electric stove and a hulking black curlicued coal stove that Betty only recognized from pictures she'd seen in children's books. Here too there were toys scattered around. A large pot bubbled at the back of the electric stove, a roast was cooking in its oven. The coal stove had a philodendron on it. There was a baby in a high chair. He was leaning over looking at the floor, and Beatrice in passing picked up the spoon he'd dropped and handed it back to him. He promptly put it in his mouth. "Woojums," said Beatrice, patting his head. "My sister Cora's baby. Mama, where are you?"

"In the dining room. No, here I am."

Mrs. Roman came in to them, large, florid, faintly jolly. She was wearing a percale housedress and an apron. "So," she said. "Betty Wilder. Beatrice has told me all about you. How you met and all. And here you are." She smiled and the jolly look deepened and possessed her face. It did not erase another, underlying, look of firmness.

"How do you do?" Betty said formally. She glanced at Clifton, who was frowning, looked back to Mrs. Roman. "I think it's so nice of you to ask me."

"Oh, a pleasure, a pleasure," said Mrs. Roman. But she looked perplexed.

My mother, thought Betty, thinks I get along with everybody. She thinks, because she's told me so, that I'd be at home anywhere. But prigs are not at home anywhere. They stop themselves from being. They're so concerned about the plumage that they quite forget the bird. That was a quotation from something, but she couldn't place it. Well, of course Mother doesn't know that I'm a prig, a snob. Nobody does. Except maybe Carol, a little bit. And since she's the same sort of snob herself, it never ruffled our relationship.

But I do not want Clifton to know, she thought mournfully. He's so easy and amiable. He's such a harmonious person. Would he understand that you can be a snob in spite of yourself? That you can hate a cluttered, seedy, hard-up house like this without wanting to? That you could dislike yourself for not liking it and yet be unable to change? No, she rather thought that Clifton would not understand. She felt in him a quality of accepting people without provisos. He would not comprehend snobbery, willful or unwilling.

I can try to be better, she thought. If I love Clifton, and I'm so very sure that I do, I can try to behave in a way that will not bring that frown to his face. In a way that will please and move him. I made a good start with Mother in the kitchen. I can keep on.

Consciously, she sought a friendly phrase and for a stricken moment thought that none would occur to her, that in this silence, stiff and clumsy, she would remain until the time for leavetaking arrived, and that then she would go, still clumsy and stiff in her pride, unlamented by the Romans or Clifton. Why should they, in the warmth and security of their friendliness, their indifference to surroundings, trouble about a cold girl once she'd gone?

Her desperate eyes found the baby, and she said,

"He's beautiful. Or is he a girl?"

Beatrice laughed. "He's a boy. He's the boy of boys, isn't he, Mama?"

"The devil of devils, you mean."

They brimmed with the baby's praises, and, praising and responding, Betty was carried past the gaping moment. After that it was easier, because they all talked so much, and more of them kept coming, slamming in through various doors and almost, it seemed, through windows. At least, a large marmalade cat came in a window, and Betty said, "What a marvelous *cat*," making a real convert to her side in the person of young Jack, who appeared from the hall just as the cat appeared on the sill.

"He's mine," said Jack.

"Well, you're lucky," Betty said, wincing a little as the cat walked delicately down the sideboard and settled beside the breadbox. "He certainly has a fine stand of whiskers," she said hastily.

Jack laughed and picked up his pet. "Caruso, I call him. He has a fine voice, too."

There were, besides Mrs. Roman, Beatrice, Jack and the baby, a four-year-old Parm (real name, Paul), a seven-year-old Gilda, an eleven-year-old Harry, and Gil, who looked to be about twenty and came in late, asking for dinner. He had a bunch of disheveled chrysanthemums for his mother, a pat for the baby, and a high-handed air that Betty didn't take to. They were all black-haired, gray-eyed and handsome. Beatrice and the baby were beautiful.

"Dinner," Mrs. Roman said, beginning to bustle. "Soon as I get the rolls in and the table set, Gil." But Gil and Cliff had gone off to another room to look at blueprints. "You, Harry—finish setting the table for Mama, okay? And Bea, I don't need you now, take your guest into the parlor, you can talk. Gilda, you want to be a big girl, help Mama get dinner ready? Parm, go call Grandma. . . ."

She swept people here and there, she ordered, directed, told Betty it was pot-luck, and sailed out to the dining room.

Bewildered, Betty followed Beatrice into the parlor.

Here was the same clutter, but here it was orderly grown-up clutter, a matter of too much of everything rather than the jumble of toys and carelessly strewn articles of clothing. There were too many claw-footed heavy pieces of furniture, too much marbling in the imitation-marble mantel, too many antimacassars and potted plants and statuettes and framed photographs. Too many draperies and too many flowers in the flowered rug.

Betty sank into a green tapestried chair and said to Beatrice, "I didn't plan to have dinner." That made an ungracious sound. "I mean, do you have enough? Did you remember about dinner when you asked me?"

"Well, I knew we'd be having it," Beatrice said, puzzled. "Oh, I see. You have dinner in the evening, I expect." Betty nodded. "We're old-fashioned, I guess. Sunday dinner in the middle of the day, always. Papa expected it."

There had been no sign of a Mr. Roman.

"Is he dead?" Betty asked carefully.

Sorrow gently touched Beatrice's face. You could see that it was an intense sorrow, but an old one, past its prime. "Three years ago," she said. "Or I wouldn't be working in that drugstore. Not that I mind, really, except that working all the time leaves you with a rather skinny social life."

"You don't have many dates?"

"Many? I don't have any. Still," she said, brightening, "I *am* going to finish high school. Mama and Gil insisted. I might have had to quit, like Cliff. Not that he minded, but I would."

"He didn't?" Betty asked, as though she hadn't heard her parents discuss this very thing. Any chance to speak of Cliff was not lightly to be lost. Besides, she could not accept Cliff's indifference to schooling. She wanted someone to tell her he'd really minded, that he'd quit under protest, only because he had to. What I want, she realized, is to find out that he's going to school at night. Working toward a Ph.D., you snob? she asked herself scornfully.

Beatrice laughed. "Cliff Banks hated school from the first day he went. I know, because he and Gil were

56

together. And Cliff was always playing hookey and leading Gil into error. Papa used to say so. Not that Papa didn't like Cliff. mind He just thought he shouldn't lead Gil into the error of hookey. Myself, I don't think Gil took much leading, but he did finish high school because Papa made him. Papa was a strong man, and he had to be When Cliff quit, Gil quit too, and Papa just took him by the ear and marched him back and that was that Gil was big then, too. But no match for Papa, Mr Roman's daughter finished proudly.

Betty had a feeling that she knew Mr. Roman. She had a feeling of being in the center of the Roman family without having gone through the preliminaries of getting to know them. She could hear Parm yelling, and knew it was Parm and not one of the other children. She heard Gilda bossing Harry and Harry bossing Jack and all of them talking at once as if she'd been hearing this sequence all her life.

She felt uncomfortable, put-upon, she didn't like this parlor and she didn't want her dinner in the middle of the day. But she felt as if she'd known these people forever. It's certainly nothing *I've* done, she told herself ruefully. I'm not relaxed or spontaneous enough to get to know people so quickly. No matter what my mother and father think. Therefore, it had to be Beatrice. It had to be the Romans themselves. You started for their house, expecting . . . what? Well, she had started expecting nothing. She hadn't even been thinking of them. She'd been thinking only of Cliff, only of the goosegirl arriving at the castle (one girl's castle is another girl's Chevvy truck, she'd say when she wrote to Carol). You started, not thinking of them, and then you turned into their blowzy depressing street, rang their chimy doorbell, and there you were, in the middle of their lives, as if you'd always been there.

Gil, at the door, said, "Okay, girls. Dinner."

He may have been merely in a hurry, or naturally terse, but to Betty he sounded peremptory, and in a state of resentment she followed Beatrice into the dining room.

5

AND THEN SHE DIDN'T SEE Cliff, not to talk to, for over two weeks. He'd go by in the truck and wave and keep going. One morning, as she waited on the highway for the school bus, he came along, slowed a little as if he might stop, but then merely nodded and went on. She saw him that same afternoon when she went to his mother's fruit stand to buy the makings of a fruit compote (her father's favorite dessert, and he was getting home that day), but Cliff was busy carrying gallons of cider from the truck and he scarely grunted a greeting.

Her heart started up in a tumult still when she saw him, and still at night she watched and waited for the truck to appear in his driveway, but it was all sad and distant. Something she had wanted very much, which might have been hers, was lost, and it was her own fault. She had tried, that day at the Romans', tried and failed to seem at ease and friendly, to seem one of them, and though they had all courteously accepted her masquerade, their eyes, as she left, said they had not been fooled.

Clifton, especially, had not been fooled.

Very well, thought Betty, walking home with the fruit that afternoon. Very well. I've lost. I love him, but I wouldn't have thought he'd be so perceptive. I underestimated him. Is that true love? she asked herself, but could only answer that she was sure the love she felt for Cliff was a true one. It was her relationship with the Romans that had been untrue. Which meant, of course, if she wanted to examine it (she did not, but somehow had to), that her relationship with anybody, including Cliff, was in some fashion wrong, at fault. Good people, real people, didn't judge by surroundings. Which leaves me where? she wondered bitterly.

Since this much introspection was all—was more—than she could tolerate, she took a deep breath and walked more quickly. She could outdistance these thoughts. At home were her parents, who loved and admired her. She'd had letters that morning from both Carol and George, who said it was dreadful without her.

"I have to admit it," Carol had written, "things just aren't the same, and I wish your father would get transferred back, though I suppose you're in a *whirl* in the East and wouldn't come back for anything. I sort of go around with Gertrude now, but she doesn't have your knack with people and she doesn't giggle, the way we used to. My, how long since I've had a good giggle. Loads of people ask for you. If you want, I'll make up a list, but it really is practically everybody. And *who* do you think turned up again? Weldon. He's aged ten years and it's most becoming. . . ."

Well, that had been all about Betty, but she'd read the comforting words several times. George had been even nicer.

"Honeybunch, I miss you like crazy. I find myself staring through the old microscope, wishing I could find you on the field. I'd pick you off with my

59

tweezers, and put you on the floor, and you'd grow into a life-sized you and I'd take you to a movie and hold your hand. After all, as I said to myself the minute you left, an amoeba is all right in its place, but it doesn't have a hand to hold. It doesn't have a brain or a heart. Honestly, there are times when I think I'd rather discover you than an amoeba capable of forming opinions and lasting affections. . . ."

Oh, there are people who are fond of me, all right. Who think I'm good and kind and loving. Why should I care what Cliff Banks thinks? She argued with herself all the way home, and won. At least, she thought, with a satirical ghost of the giggle Carol had liked, the part of me that *likes* me has won. That other part, that carping other Betty who finds faults with my motives and admires Clifton for finding them askew, is defeated. I put Clifton Banks out of my mind once before. This time it should be easier.

She thought about her letters, and wondered if maybe next summer she could make a trip to Chicago, to see the people who valued her.

Then her father, who'd arrived in her absence, jumped up with such pleasure at the sight of her that Betty, who for all her inner arguing had felt raw and hurt and insecure for days, was suddenly at peace.

I'm my kind of person, she decided, kissing her father and asking warmly, interestedly, how the first trip had been. Maybe it's not a perfect kind, maybe not good enough for sensitive, perceptive, choosy Clifton Banks, but a lot of people like me and, furthermore, I like myself. Which means I can't love Clifton. There could never be a question of love between two such different people.

So there.

"Daddy, you're looking marvelous. What did you do, sell fifty thousand copies of *The Cart Before the Horse*?"

"That'll be the day," he laughed. "The day I sell two copies of that, I'll take you and your mother around the world. No lesser celebration would be in order."

"Darling, bring the fruit in here," Mrs. Wilder called.

60

"I want to get everything ready, and then we can all sit down and have a nice talk."

They went into the kitchen and the three of them stayed together talking while Mrs. Wilder prepared dinner. Betty felt cloaked with affection, unassailable, proof against anyone's criticism, Clifton's or her own. She never looked that evening at all to see if his truck was there in the driveway. Once she glanced toward the window, but all she said was, "It gets dark earlier and earlier."

"It's good to be home, in our house, on an early autumn evening," said Mr. Wilder. "Say, do you think it's too warm to light a fire? You haven't had one yet, have you?"

"Of course not," said Mrs. Wilder. "We've been waiting for you. But it is a little warm," she added.

"We'll open the door," said Betty. "This is Daddy's first night, so we should have our first fire."

So after dinner Mr. Wilder laid a precise and cozy fire, lit it, and they sat, talking, falling silent, thinking their thoughts.

Betty preferred this school to the one in Chicago. That had been a king of uglies. Of course, she'd got used to it, accustomed to the peeling saffron paint, the big, old-fashioned, smelly washrooms, the never adequately heated gymnasium, the high-ceilinged echoing cafeteria with its scarred tables and cracked tile walls. She'd hated and then forgotten the air that seemed filtered through chalk-powder and disinfectant, the way rain strung down the windows in smeared and dirty beads, the way the change bells rang like shrieks of pain every forty minutes. She'd been happy in school, and so had been able to forget what it looked like.

But the school here in Norwood was beautiful and new. Which is nice, she thought a bit grimly, since I certainly wouldn't describe myself as frantically happy within its walls. It was a rambling modern place, only two stories high, endlessly windowed. And the windows were always clean. The walls were painted in soft pastels. In the gymnasium everything was fresh and clean—ropes, baskets, tumbling mats, balls, white lines on the floor. The cafeteria was pretty and light and had a garden planted just outside the wall that was one huge window. The change bells were soft, and even chalk didn't squeak on the blackboards here. Here were fresh maps and clean books and a library where you weren't powdered with the dust of years the moment you entered.

Even the teachers looked fresher here, and why would they not? Probably they weren't any better than the teachers in Chicago, but, like the library, the teachers in Chicago had been vaguely obscured by dust. And so were we all, thought Betty, who could wear a blouse here three or four times without washing it, and who didn't feel she needed a bath as soon as she got home.

"I don't want to make you jealous," she wrote Carol, "but honestly, this school is the most. In looks, I mean. I haven't met a teacher yet as good as Miss Rory was in Latin—give her my love, won't you—but they're good enough and the building is out of this world. Shining, gleaming, bright as a mirror, and I mean it. I've met some nice people. Especially a girl named Beatrice Roman. Of course, she isn't you, but she's very nice. She hasn't giggled yet, but maybe she does with other people. I mean, don't you feel you have to know someone awfully well to giggle with them? And then, you have to think the same things are funny. I don't know her that well yet." She paused, wondering whether to add that it looked as if she might never know Beatrice that well. No point, really. "Nothing especially interesting in the male line." She paused again, went on doggedly. "Not yet, that is. Time enough. I had something I was worried about, but I like the school and our house so much that I've completely mislaid it and am not about to make a search."

That was the only reference she made to Clifton, or her own self-doubts. It's not a completely honest letter, she thought, but what am I to do?

The mornings now were warm, but with a gingery flick of autumn in the smell of leaves and the mild wind's breath. Betty, after breakfast, would tie the sleeves of a cardigan around her shoulders, pick up her books, walk down to the highway to wait for the school bus. That in itself was a new experience.

Apprehensive, sure she'd be late, she'd left the first morning so early that she had to wait twenty minutes. She'd sat on an old orchard wall, on a big flat stone, and listened to the soft wind in dry leaves, watched the traffic pass, watched flocks of birds she could not identify wheeling in the great tender blue sky. Migrating, she thought, and considered for a while how powerful their wings must be.

To her astonished delight, a small rabbit hopped across the orchard, through the dry grass, almost to where she sat. Then he spied her and sat up abruptly, little feet hanging against his snowy chest, whiskers convulsed, ears steady as stone, and gave her a long dubious glance. He wheeled, but without apparent alarm, and started back in the direction from which he'd come, long legs thrusting leisurely up and down.

"Toodle-oo," Betty said to the white salaam of his tail.

The bus came, and she rose, waving so it would be sure to stop, and got aboard. The driver, a cross-looking small man, gave her an extremely sweet smile. He was very quiet, but the bus was as noisy as the stockyards, and for a moment Betty, blank-eyed with nervousness, could not find a place to sit, but then she did, next to a girl with braids who looked about ten and was leaning over a miserably smudged—probably even tear-smudged—arithmetic book. The appearance of that book, broken-spined and dog-eared, took Betty back, and she remembered weeping over arithmetic . . . heavens, how long ago. She liked times when, without forewarning, she was suddenly thrust into her own past, even her own weepy past, because now it was all over and she could indulge a wistful moment without being hurt. Crackerjacks could do it, and the little favor that came in crackerjack boxes. That always carried her over the years to a point where she met her small self burrowing stickily for the paper-wrapped prize—a little delicate top, a toy soldier, a beetle-shaped tin thing that popped pleasingly. And library paste could induce this nostalgia. Paste that was white and creamy in the center, and at the edges yellowed a bit and split. She would see it, smell its sharp thin odor, and once again she was pasting lace on paper hearts. And she'd always wanted to eat it, and sometimes still did want to.

Pleased by the rabbit and her own nostalgia, she arrived quite happily that first morning. After that, as she told herself several days later, the deluge. But still she spoke more wryly than unhappily, and still she was not seriously alarmed.

It was several mornings before she encountered Beatrice, and then by accident. She had to call over several intervening heads. "Hi, Beatrice . . . wait up."

"Well, hi," said Beatrice, with her light lovely smile. "Guess we don't have any classes together."

"No, and I'm sorry. When do you have lunch?" She was surprised at the eagerness in her own voice.

"One o'clock."

"So do I. Funny we haven't met."

They were walking down a long corridor to the place where the lockers were, and at every other step Beatrice was greeted, detained, smiled at. The way I used to be, Betty thought, with a touch of depression. And then, Oh, well, it'll be that way here, too. I just don't know anyone yet. She could not help thinking that Beatrice, even though she said she didn't have a social life, certainly knew everyone.

"I go over to Perkins' for lunch," Beatrice explained. "He gives it to me and I sort of give the other girl a hand with sodas and stuff."

"Not a very relaxed way to have lunch, is it?"

Beatrice shrugged. "Can't be helped. Anyway, I'm not the relaxing type." The bell rang. "Where're you off to now?"

"Down there." Betty gestured back along the endless corridor. "Science."

"I'm going up." At the foot of the stairway, Beatrice hesitated. "You all right here? Getting to know people and all?"

"I'm fine."

Walking toward the science room, Betty reflected that in actual fact she was not so very fine, and getting to know people wasn't proving as easy as she'd expected. But Beatrice hadn't said anything very detaining, hadn't suggested any meetings, so I'm fine was the only possible answer to make her. You had your pride, after all.

Anyway, she wasn't anxious. After all these years of getting along with people, of being popular, there was no reason to suppose that she'd suddenly become a pariah. She recalled quite clearly that in Chicago, where she'd practically grown up with all the students around her, they'd wait awhile, sizing up new people before making a move either toward or away from them. You were busy with your own group, your own particular friends, and a new person took some thinking over, that was all. So, presumably, she was being thought over here. For her own part, she was not too eager to rush into anything. A few words, a nod or a smile here and there was all right, but she'd seen too many people make mistakes just because they *had* to get assimilated right away. When Christine had first come to the Chicago school, she'd almost died of gratitude because that awful Jorman girl paid some attention to her, and the first thing she knew she was almost irretrievably tangled in the Jorman web of artsy-folksy girls and cipher-like boys who were there but never really quite with it. It was sheer fluke that Carol had discovered her, and, except for Carol, she probably would have finished out her school career with that but utterly nil crowd. Or else she'd have dropped them and been nowhere. Betty had known that to happen, too.

Therefore, you waited. You answered when spoken to, but not too effusively, smiled when smiled at, but not too wishfully. In time you found a place that fitted you, your special niche in the world of high school.

At this time, Betty was so preoccupied with Clifton Banks, her mind and heart so filled with his image, that being peacefully indifferent to the effect she made in school was simple. Clifton puzzled, absorbed, and pained her, but now and then she had a moment of gratitude toward him. To spend the last year of high school in a strange place would be difficult for the most self-confident girl, and Betty, though she had self-confidence, did not have the most. Cliff removed nearly all the sting from that situation by being an even sharper thorn.

The days passed, and slowly she came to know names, faces, to lose from one room after another, one street after another, that sense of challenge that new places flaunt but cannot keep. She no longer lost her way in the shining labyrinth of Norwood High School. She could find her way home from almost any part of town, in two or three different ways. When she walked downtown an occasional "Hi" (unaccompanied by her name yet, it was true) would greet her. She and her mother no longer said home when they meant Chicago. They said Chicago. And when Mr. Wilder got back from the first swing around his new territory, he took off his hat and said, "Oof . . . it's good to be home."

It hadn't taken very long.

"So you ride the school bus, do you?" Mr. Wilder asked Betty that first evening as they sat around the fire that was too hot even with the doors and windows open (but none of them would admit it). "Do you like it? I've never ridden in one."

"It's all right. Noisy, you know. And people tend to throw things around. But you get used to it."

"And the school? How do you like the school?"

"Palatial," said Betty. "It took me a while to find my way around, because it's so spread out. But I think it's gorgeous. They're going to have an open house for parents next month. Maybe you can go, if you're here."

Mr. Wilder hitched his chair a little away from the fire. "Chances are I will be. I won't be away from home nearly as much now." He shook his head wonderingly, as if he didn't believe it yet. "Sometimes I think to myself that if I see one more hotel room, one more menu under a glass-topped desk, one bellboy . . . just one . . ." He stopped. "I may very well be here for the open house, honey. I'll look forward to it. Phone begun to ring all the time?" At a glance from his wife, he coughed and said, "Hardly time yet, of course . . ."

Betty laughed. "Daddy, don't be tactful with me. It makes me nervous."

"Well, I only meant . . . Say, this fire is pretty, isn't it?"

"Beautiful," said Mrs. Wilder. "Our first fire." And she, too, moved back from it. "Draws well. The mantel, I mean."

Her husband snorted with amusement. "It isn't the mantel that draws, dear. It's the flue."

"Whatever it is that keeps a fire going briskly, ours is doing it admirably."

Betty closed the fire screen, which cut off some of the heat, and sat well back.

"How's young Banks?" Mr. Wilder asked after a pause.

Mrs. Wilder glanced at Betty, who appeared to be lost in a study of the flames. "He seems well," she said. "We don't see much of him. So busy, I guess."

So as to make it seem unimportant, Betty said, "He drove me over to Bea's one day. We had a talk, of sorts. Nothing interesting."

"I see," her father said. "Who's Bea?"

"Beatrice Roman. A girl I met. Awfully nice. But she's pretty busy, too. Works in a drugstore and has an enormous family that she has to help take care of. Their father is dead, and there are an awful lot of children. So Bea is kept pretty busy."

"I see," said Mr. Wilder again. Their earlier mood of cozy, happy comfort seemed to be dispersing, and Mr. Wilder would not have it so. "We could pop some corn," he said. "Except that I won't get any closer to that fire than I already am. Who suggested a fire, anyway?"

Betty and Mrs. Wilder laughed, and as easily as that the mood was recaptured. It's because we're all so willing, Betty thought, liking her parents and herself for the willingness.

The fire, from a distance, was lovely, was what her father had meant it to be, a symbol of something close, a ceremony for a beginning. They sat around it, as families had sat around fires for thousands of years, and felt in this way a sort of alliance that did not need words. Now actually forgetful of school and Clifton, Betty sat with her arms clasped around her knees, and was glad that she was with her mother and father. There were times when her mother angered and vexed her, times when she thought her father let her down, but the fact, in this firelight, was clear—she loved her parents.

She knew people who did not.

Carol didn't care for her mother. "I mean," she'd say, "we're stuck with each other, and for the present there's nothing either one of us can do about it, but the day I can, I mean the very *first* day, I'm going to leave so fast there'll be nothing but a blur in the air as I go by."

"What are you going to do then?" Betty had asked curiously.

"Work, what else? Or else the blond young millionaire will come riding from all directions and sweep me off my feet."

"When is all this going to be?"

"How do I know? When I'm through with school, I suppose."

"Quite a long way off. Seems to me that if you go on feeling this way, maybe your mother won't want to support you till then."

"I don't believe it has much to do with want," Carol had replied coldly. "She has to. It's in the fine print, or something."

Carol's mother had been married three times. Her present husband was an F.B.I. man who looked exceedingly grouchy, and was. "How do you feel about your father?" Betty had asked that day.

"Which?" said Carol. "This step, or the last step, or the real one back in the mists of time? Don't specify. I don't like any of them."

"Not even the real one?" Betty had asked.

"I don't like him the most of all. Do you know that from the day he walked out of the house I've never heard another *word* from him? He's never once written, or tried to find out how I am, or what I am, or anything about me. He's the worst. At least there was nothing in that fine print said these other two had to like me. But *him*. Don't talk to me about him."

Betty did know all that, but it seemed to give Carol satisfaction to repeat the cold mean facts from time to time. As if, thought Betty, repetition would one day either change the facts or make them finally acceptable. She had an idea, upon which she could not act because she didn't know how, that Carol sort of wanted her to defend that seemingly indefensible father. But what in the world could you say in his behalf?

No, Carol didn't like her parents, but Carol had reason. On the other hand, George didn't much care for his, and he had no reason at all. His were nice people, affectionate, anxious, concerned. They did everything they could—they really did more than they could—for this indifferent son. And it wasn't anything so definite as outright dislike or rebellion that George showed them. He simply ignored them. Took what they offered—care, money, fondness—as if it were all being served from a tray in the air. Of course, George was not unique. Lots of people in their teens became suddenly impatient with their parents. Maybe it was a matter of having been dependent for so long, and now in the flush of that first glimpse of yourself as a grown, independent being, you just didn't stop to think of the people you were growing away from. You saw yourself free . . . on the verge of anything and everything, strong enough for all of it. You practically said, Anything you can offer, World, I can take. But the thing was, you had to keep your eyes on that vision every second. One glance to right or left, one quick look behind, and your balance was gone, and there you were, back in the old dependency. Oh, I can see what they mean, she thought, George and the people like him.

Only I'm glad I'm me. Perfectly willing to grow up, but not breaking my neck over it. "There's plenty of time," I used to say to George, but he'd say, "No, no, no, there isn't. Do you realize, do you ever stop to *think* how short a span mankind has? It makes me furious, thinking of all those idiotic parrots and turtles living for hundreds of years and we have our little threescore, and so much to do in it. What do you mean, there's plenty of time? There's barely time to get started."

"I guess," she'd replied weakly, "I don't have anything special I want to do."

"Oh, you're hopeless. Are you going to sit there and tell me you don't want to do anything?"

"No, because that isn't what I said. I have lots of plans, sort of. I'm going to do lots of things. I even know some things I'm not going to do. But I'm just not in a tailspin, that's all. I'm having fun, George."

"Fun doing what?" he yelled.

"Oh . . . dates, dances. Ball games. I think it's fun looking in your microscope." She knew that would irritate him, and it did.

"Fun," he said scornfully. "Betty Wilder, I want to inform you that I consider you frivolous and feather-brained, and the only reason I have anything to do with you at all is that you're pretty."

"That's awfully nice of you, George. Do turtles and parrots really live hundreds of years?"

She smiled now, remembering the look on his face.

"Something funny?" said her father.

"Oh, I was just remembering something George said one day."

"How is he? Have you heard from him?"

"I had a letter today. He says he'd rather see me than discover an amoeba capable of forming opinions and lasting affections."

"The boy's obviously half mad with grief."

"Oh, very likely," said Betty with a smile. "Being the sentimental type he is."

"I'd sentimental him, if I were his mother," Mrs. Wilder said darkly.

Betty, who was willing to criticize her contemporaries in her own mind, or even with another of her contemporaries, was not willing to share such views with her parents. She stretched and said the first thing that came to mind. "Should we put another log on the fire?"

Mr. Wilder's eyebrows rose in alarm. "Over my dead —from heat exhaustion—body, you'll put another log on that fire."

Yet it was lovely. Tender and bright, it branched up the chimney with a soft roar, and they could not take their eyes from it.

6

"I MIGHT AS WELL TELL YOU now," Betty wrote to Carol, "since I'm all over it, but for about fifteen or twenty minutes there, I was madly in love. This, I said to myself, is the real thing, the absolute, the end. His name was—I mean is, he no longer exists for me but I guess that doesn't relegate him to the past tense—Clifton Banks. He is handsome, happy, industrious, sort of wistful perhaps. He has a sort of bronze voice, and blue, blue, blue eyes. I knew when I looked at him that this was love. The way, if you'd never seen a diamond, then someone showed you one, you'd know right away that this was a diamond. And he? Oh, he does not, and did not, for a moment, love me. I think he thinks I'm a smug snob. Which you know is not the case. A snob, maybe, sort of. Smug—no. I think, come to think of it, he doesn't think anything of or about me at all. He is, as I say, sober and industrious and cheerful. It sounds awful, but it's really a lovely combination when it looks like Cliff. It's a splendid combination if you're the right type girl, but if not, not. I'm not. . . ."

She stopped, because the letter was beginning to feel a bit repetitious. Too many thinks and nots. She wasn't at all sure she wanted to write it. . . .

She tried never to think of that Sunday at the Romans'. It wasn't a shameful memory. She had nothing to reproach herself with. Well, perhaps there was a little something to reproach herself with. But not much. A matter of being . . . Possibly she'd been a little ungracious. But not very, and it was not of much moment. She just didn't particularly care for the recollection. Yet she would think of it with the same uncomfortable nagging concern she felt when a faint blemish seemed to be appearing on her skin. She'd look at it, decide it was nothing, it would go away, she'd ignore it, and then she'd be back at the mirror, staring intently, with a sinking heart. Was it going away? Was it getting worse?

What *had* she done wrong at the Romans', that great family with all the gusto and gestures that her own family did without?

She had not much cared for Gil Roman, but that was immaterial. She hadn't shown it. Even if she had, there seemed to be very little chance that anyone would notice, since the entire family was so intent on talking that they'd probably not have noticed if she'd got down on the floor and played with Caruso's catnip mouse. So surely the fault, if fault there was, lay with them in their manner of so completely accepting a person that she all but disappeared in their midst. If you're a guest, people are supposed to pay attention to you, are they not? And did the Romans pay attention to her that day? They did not. That was, she amended testily, no special, guest-like attentions were paid her. Probably you could interpret it as flattering, and even attribute it to the special bouquet of your own personality. Except that she couldn't for a moment think the Romans' attitude toward her was different from their attitude toward anyone. They took everything just this casually.

From Parm (and, for all she knew, Vernon, the baby) on up, these people took what came their way and expected it to fit their way.

They had all (Betty was past counting) sat at a big round dining-room table. The baby, next to Beatrice in a high chair, was not fed but just sat making an unattractive mess of a piece of zwieback. Grandma—Mrs. Roman senior—sat beside Beatrice. She was almost as small as Gilda, and had a way of tipping her eyes up when she spoke that made Betty feel as if she were on a ladder.

There had been a tremendous tureen of stew, two long loaves of warm crusty bread, a wooden bowl of tossed green salad, an assortment of preserves, and, on the sideboard, a great coconut layer cake. Betty had looked at all this, miserably conscious of having had a good breakfast.

Mrs. Roman dished up a trencherman's helping of stew, and Grandma was served. Filling another plate, she indicated Betty with a smile. Gil began to pass it to her.

"Oh, but I couldn't—" Betty said.

"Nonsense, nonsense," said Mrs. Roman, happy to press her. "Eat it up. You're too thin."

I am not too thin. "But I just—practically just had breakfast. Really, I couldn't."

Mrs. Roman had looked at her, momentarily baffled by sincerity in what she had taken to be a courteous first protest. Gil, looking resigned, still held the plate midway between his mother and the girl who was holding things up. The rest of the family watched with interest, and Harry took advantage of the short silence to announce that he'd made up a joke.

Gilda obligingly asked what it was.

"If an oyster," said Harry, "makes a pearl and then refuses to give it up, would you call him shellfish?"

There was laughter, but Gilda merely looked bewildered. "I don't get it."

"How *about* it?" said Gil, who was still holding the plate.

"No, really—" Betty's face warmed, and she wished desperately that she'd said nothing.

Gil put the plate down before him. "Okay. I'll eat it myself."

Mrs. Roman served another dish, and if there was any difference in the helping, it was not apparent to Betty. "Better?" Mrs. Roman said cheerfully, handing it to Gil and once again indicating Betty.

"Thank you," said Betty. She'd have to do what she could. She avoided looking at Clifton, and wondered why in the world she should feel defensive. There were the old laws about breaking bread with friends, but your stomach had laws of its own.

"You ain't hungry?" said Harry kindly, ignoring Gilda, who was pulling at his sleeve.

"Aren't," said Beatrice. "She isn't."

"Pity," said Harry. "Stop it, Gilda." He looked at his mother, impatient for everyone to be served.

"Who is she?" said Parm, his big sober eyes fixed on Betty.

"A friend of mine, dear," Beatrice explained. "Betty, her name is."

"Hi," said Parm, and scowled at Gilda, who'd apparently lost interest in Harry and was reaching for the pickle dish. "Don't take pickles yet. It ain't time."

"Isn't," said Beatrice. "It isn't time."

"See?" said Parm to his sister in triumph.

"Shut up," said Gilda.

When they were all served, Betty picked up her fork, put it down immediately while Gil said grace.

"I thought you weren't hungry," Gilda said.

Betty looked at her helplessly, wondering if you explained to someone her age that you were not hungry, you'd merely wanted not to seem reluctant. She realized what a handicap it was to have had experience only of people your own age or your parents' age. No one younger, no one older, just about no one in between. She had no recollection at all of her own grandparents, and how, being an only child, would she know anything of younger children? Baby-sitting, perhaps. But in Chicago she hadn't done any of that, and though she'd wondered idly if she might try in Norwood, this hour with the assorted Roman children had so alarmed her that she was sure she'd never try now.

"Pass the pickles," said Harry. Gilda again was tugging at his arm.

"Please," said Mrs. Roman.

"Yeah. Please. Anyway, pass them. Gilda, what do you want?"

"I don't see your joke," she complained.

"Cliff," said Gil, "I told Moore we'd be there at two sharp."

"That's okay," said Cliff. "We'll make it. This is good, Mrs. Roman. Pass the bread."

"Please," said Beatrice.

Cliff laughed. "Excuse me. I do mean please. Comes of being around Harry so much. I lost my manners."

Harry paid no attention. He was trying to explain the intricacies of his joke to Gilda.

"What's lost?" said Grandma. "Jack's looking for lost things." She smacked her lips as she ate, and Betty had been trying not to hear her, but she heard this and wondered if she'd missed something.

"Oh, yeah. The lost articles." Gil snorted. "He goes around, Cliff, with his eyes on the sidewalk, looking for these things people advertise that are lost. What's one of them, Jack, boy?"

Jack, not at all put out, said, "One's an earring. Gold, studied with emeralds and rubies—"

"Studded," said Beatrice. "Not studied."

"Studded," Jack agreed. "Another's a lady's cocktail watch—whatever that is—braided platinum band and diamonds, liberal reward—"

"Jack," said Mrs. Roman severely, "I don't mind you going around with your nose in the ground looking, but rewards for being honest you don't take. Understand? You find something, you return it, period. No rewards."

"No rewards!" Jack yelled indignantly. "What's the point in finding it if I don't get the reward?"

"Honesty is its own reward."

"Listen," Jack said, so tensely that his economy might have been facing a real threat, "if this lady is dumb enough to lose her cocktail watch with platinum braided band and diamonds, she *ought* to pay a reward, to teach her a lesson. How do you know she won't go and lose it again, if she don't get taught a lesson?"

"So that's why you'd take the reward?" Gil said, a smile twitching at his lips. "To improve the lady's character?"

"Oh, you dry up." Jack turned again to his mother and said, "No, but listen, Mama—"

"No listens about it," said Mrs. Roman. "You don't take rewards for being honest, and that's that."

"Oh, I'll be darned," Jack said furiously, glaring around the table. His glare took in everyone and moved down to include Caruso on the floor. "I'll just be darned."

"If you give me the socks," said Grandma to Mrs. Roman, "I'll darn them after dinner for you. I ain't got anything else to do."

Betty stifled a giggle and tried to eat. As Cliff said, the stew was good. And it was so too much. She swallowed, moved some vegetables to another part of the plate, put a carrot in her mouth and chewed some more.

"I thought Cora said she was going to come for Woojums before dinner," Beatrice said. "I hope she doesn't expect me to take care of him. I've got a guest."

Well, at least she remembers, Betty thought. I really thought she'd forgotten I was here. She speared a potato, sighed inaudibly, and went to work on it. Would it be worse to be named Vernon or nicknamed Woojums? How long would he *be* Woojums? Up to six might be all right, even maybe till eight, but much past that and—

"Cora'll be along for him, all right," said Mrs. Roman easily. "Cliff, you ready for seconds? No? Anybody? Pass your plate, then, Jack, and stop sulking. Honesty is its own—"

The front door banged open, banged shut, a clear voice called, "Hi, hi, hi . . . where is everyone? Oh, here you are, of course. And here's my Wooj—Wooj—Woojums. . . ."

Cora, another unmistakable Roman, sailed in smiling and laughing. "Honestly, that *man* of mine. He's out in the car. He won't come in. He says to tell you all Sunday is a day of rest and his idea of rest is not the Romans at Sunday dinner."

Everyone laughed. But Betty felt a wave of fellow feeling for that man of Cora's, prudently waiting outside in the car.

Cora dashed into the kitchen, came back with a cloth to wipe Vernon's becrumbed face, picked him up in her arms, and said, "So long, everybody. Thanks oodles for taking my lamb chop here. Has he been an angel?"

As she went out the door, two or three people assured her that Woojums had been an angel. The front door banged and she was gone.

"My," said Mrs. Roman, with a sigh. "It always seems lonesome when Vernon goes, doesn't it?"

Betty choked.

"Something wrong with this girl?" said Grandma. "She chokes. She don't eat. She don't talk. Something wrong with her?"

Every eye was on Betty, who was clutched first by stage fright, then anger, then a weak longing to be home. "I . . ." She managed a laugh that sounded, in her own ears, like a cackle. "Must have swallowed something the wrong way." Let me *alone*.

"You weren't eating," Parm pointed out carefully.

You little pill. "I was. You just weren't looking closely. I—"

"Hey, now. Cut it out, everyone," Beatrice said hotly. "Betty'll think we don't have any manners."

"What do you mean, think?" Jack said. Of all the people in the room, he was the only one Betty could, at that moment, stand.

"Enough of that," said Gil. "Come on, Cliff. We have to get along."

"Your cake!" said Mrs. Roman anxiously. "Bea, cut the boys some cake and get them their coffee, they're in a hurry."

"Don't hurry on my account," said Grandma. This time Betty couldn't help it, she laughed. "That's a good girl," said Grandma. "Pass the preserves."

Cliff and Gil left shortly, with only the most general good-by. Of course, Betty told herself, in a household this size they could scarcely take individual farewells, but he might at least have looked at me. She decided he was a prig, rebuked herself, decided she was a prig, changed her mind, decided she didn't know what to think except that the afternoon was not going notably well and she did not consider it altogether her own fault. They hadn't even bothered—or noticed that they hadn't bothered—to introduce her to Cora. I'm just not used, she thought fretfully, to families so big, so casual about their manners, so offhand.

She felt a wrench of longing for Chicago. For Carol and George and Christine, for the apartments she knew and the school she knew and all the things she'd left behind.

And what was she going to do now? It seemed as if she'd been here all day, but actually it had been only about an hour and a half. By no reasonable method could she extricate herself for at least another two. She'd been invited for the afternoon. She couldn't develop a toothache, or remember that her mother had said to be home by two-thirty. There was no logical, polite way to leave. And when she did leave she didn't know how to get home from here, a part of the town to which she'd never been. Clifton Banks had said nothing about taking her back, and she certainly would not have asked him.

Simply by being here, she'd found out one thing she'd wanted very much, a short while ago, to know. Beatrice and Clifton were not in love with each other. But the fact had relevance no longer. What difference who he did or didn't love, since he scarcely liked her well enough for conversation? He'd asked her for a date once. Well, and so he had. But he's not about to ask again, she told herself, and that's quite plain.

"Something bothering you?" Beatrice asked, getting up to clear the table. Grandma and the children drifted away.

"I was just wondering about how to get home." At Beatrice's glance, she said quickly, "I just meant that Cliff is gone, and all. I only wondered when I did leave, *how* I did."

"I'll get you on the bus," Beatrice assured her.

Troubled and nonplused, Betty nodded and began to help clear. She and Beatrice carried dishes into the kitchen, where Mrs. Roman competently prepared them for washing. There was no dishwasher here, but in a surprisingly short time everything was done, the kitchen in order.

"Well," said Mrs. Roman. "I'll just get a few things started for supper now, while the place is clear."

"Do you cook all the time?" Betty asked, a bit plaintively.

Mrs. Roman considered. "With a family this size, it's cook or clear up or market most of the time. Laundry and house-cleaning in between. No rest for a woman," she said cheerfully.

"Thanks for helping," Beatrice said as they went, at her suggestion, upstairs to her room. We may, she'd said, we just *may* get a little peace and quiet up there. No guarantee, of course.

"Oh, I'm glad to help," Betty said. She was being truthful. She never did mind helping in someone else's house. It was in her own that all her resistance rose up at the mention of work. "It's just . . . don't you hate housework? Watching your mother working or getting ready to work all the time? My mother doesn't work nearly as hard as yours, and I've gotten so depressed watching her over the years that I've made up my mind never to do any housework that I can possibly avoid."

Beatrice didn't reply immediately. She'd stopped at a bedroom door, looked in, sighed, and said, "What a mess. Gilda, would you mind going somewhere else for a while? I'd like to have two minutes—I mean," she corrected (Gilda was apparently a literal child), "I'd like to have some time with my guest."

The bedroom, not large, was indeed a mess. Clothing and magazines and doll furnishings were strewn about. An open box of costume jewelry was on the floor, and marmalade Caruso lay beside it entangled in a string of green glass beads that reflected his eyes. He looked indolent and wealthy. But everything else in the room was threadbare.

79

Beatrice picked a doll off one bed, transferred it to another. "Can't you keep your things on your side of the room?" she asked her sister mildly.

"Do I have to go?" Gilda asked. She was sitting beside Caruso, dangling a string of tarnished gold beads before him. Good-naturedly, he flicked them with a paw, forgot, licked his snowy chest, abandoned that and lay back in his finery, slowly waving his tail.

"Yes, you have to," Beatrice said. "And take Caruso with you, or Jack will be in here looking for him."

"What are you going to talk about that's so secret?" Gilda demanded. "I'll tell Mama. It's my room too, you know."

"On your way," said Beatrice. "You're breaking the agreement."

"I never made the agreement to start with," Gilda said conversationally. She gathered Caruso up in her arms, and the green glass beads slid slowly to the floor. "An agreement has to be made by two people, doesn't it? What's an agreement about one person deciding and telling the other person?"

"The next time you come into Perkins'," said Beatrice, "looking for a free soda, you're going to get a glass of water, without ice. And I'll charge you."

"It's blackmail," said Gilda, going to the door. "When can I come back?"

"Close the door as you leave," said Beatrice.

Gilda lingered a moment, shrugged and left, pulling the door to but not quite closing it.

Beatrice looked around the rumpled room as though deciding what to do with it. She took a skirt and sweater from a chair, held them a moment, dropped them on the bed with the doll. "Do you have any brothers or sisters? Grab that chair there before something else gets in it. I think gremlins take stuff out of the drawers and scatter it around."

Betty sat. "No," she said, in answer to Beatrice's question, "I'm an only child." She tried to make it wistful.

"Shouldn't think there'd be enough housework to get you depressed."

"Any amount depresses me. Maybe it's the *having* to do it."

"You have to breathe, too."

This seemed to Betty a faulty parallel, but she said nothing. Beatrice, propped against pillows on the bed, was quiet, too. Somewhere a radio was turned on and loudly Perry Como marched to the blues. Harry poked his head in. "Lookin' for Parm."

"Not here," said Beatrice. "Close the door, will you?"

Harry banged it shut, opened it again and said, "If you see him, tell him, huh?" and went off, leaving it open.

"Shall I?" said Betty, half rising.

"Oh, someone'll come along." Briefly, Beatrice closed her eyes. Her long lashes fluttered and were still, her usually mobile brows and mouth were still. Then the gray eyes opened and looked straight into Betty's brown ones. "Sorry, I usually go into a quick slump about this time on Sunday."

I don't blame you, Betty thought. And then, But why ask me over, when you know the slump is due? Why, she was wondering, ask me anyway? We scarcely spoke that day in the drugstore, and you'd hardly say that we'd become friends on the moment. Tentatively she wondered if Cliff might have reminded Beatrice, might have felt concerned. But that was not reasonable. You aren't concerned about someone and then lose that concern just because she's a little uneasy in a new house. But then . . . why? Why was she here?

"Don't you get tired of why?" she asked.

"Why? Tired of it?"

"I mean, I'm always asking myself why. Why did this happen, why didn't that, why are we or aren't we, why, why, why."

"I love why," Beatrice said slowly. "It leads somewhere. Usually."

Betty felt cheated, because actually she too loved why. It was only for the moment that she'd got annoyed with it, and now she'd gone and stamped herself as a person who didn't inquire, or didn't wish to. Do I have to say everything that comes into my head? she mourned, wondering if she could salvage some part of why for herself, and realizing that she could not. For the moment, it was all Beatrice's. And Beatrice had made such a nice answer, too.

Well, anyway, they were talking. She opened her mouth to say something about school, and the fat biscuit-colored dog lolled into the room, exuding a strong furry odor. He collapsed on the floor and then looked about as though wondering what he'd come for. He had a droll little face and almost no tail.

Beatrice sniffed the air. "What *does* he get into? Parm? Parm, where are you?"

"Here," said a distant voice.

"Well, I don't know where here is, but will you please come and get this animal and put him back outdoors and don't let him in again, understand?"

Parm appeared at the door and looked at his sister reproachfully. "How would *you* like to be put outdoors?"

"If I smelled like Bouncer, there, I'd expect it. Take him *away*."

"Maybe we could give him a bath," Parm said hopefully.

"Not me. See if Jack and Harry will help you."

"Okay."

Parm grabbed Bouncer's collar and half-dragged, half-helped him from the room. Bouncer slumped and whined and rolled accusing eyes backward at Beatrice.

"Oh, for heaven's sake," Beatrice said with a laugh. "Do you have any pets?" she asked Betty.

"No." Bouncer was no inducement. Of course, Caruso was lovely. Especially adorned with green glass beads (his still lay on the floor where they'd fallen). "No, we lived in an apartment in Chicago, and I guess Mother is too fussy a housekeeper to want pets. Maybe now I can have one." She didn't in the least—at the moment, anyway—want a pet, but it seemed a politic remark.

"Do you miss Chicago?" Beatrice asked.

"Well, yes. In ways. But Norwood is pretty, and of course we've never lived in a house before, and I think that's a lot of fun. Mother says—"

"Bea," said Jack, coming in quickly. "Oh, excuse me. You were talking."

Beatrice looked apologetically at Betty, turned to her brother. "It's all right. Only hurry up. Honestly, I have a guest about once a year—"

"I *said* excuse me, didn't I? After all—"

"Jack, dear. What do you want?"

"Huh? Oh . . . Well, Parm says you said to wash Bouncer, and I can't find that stuff, that whatyoucallit, that we bought to wash him with that kills fleas."

"Then don't wash him."

"But we've got him all *wet*," Jack protested.

Beatrice swung her legs around to the floor, grimaced at Betty. "Do you mind? Come on down with me while I find the stuff, will you? We can talk there."

And so the afternoon had gone, until Betty, unable to stand it any longer, had said that her mother expected her home by five. Some of them (Betty didn't know how many) had been sitting around the big kitchen table playing poker (which Betty had never played before), and for half an hour she'd been growing more and more resentful and uncomfortable. She'd been turning over in her mind certain phrases of excuse, discarding them, going back to them, making foolish plays in the card game and answering questions incoherently. Bouncer was lying against her foot, and remained there despite her furtive attempts to shove him off with the other foot. He smelled now of some exceedingly powerful soap, and his fur was still damp, and for the first time in her life Betty had a strong desire to kick an animal. She was convinced that nothing short of a kick would dislodge him. She did not like card games and could not grasp the essentials of poker. She wanted, almost frantically, to be home. And I'm *not* being ill-natured, she told herself defensively. I'm just not used to such big families, such clustering of people and animals, such . . .

"Are you going to call me?" Grandma said to her. "If you're going to call, call."

"What?" said Betty nervously. "Oh, no . . . no, sorry, I guess I can't."

"You're all going to have to clear out of here, sorry

to say." Mrs. Roman appeared at the kitchen door. "I have to start supper."

There was a general protest, and Betty took the chance to explain to Beatrice that she'd promised to be home by five.

"It's only that Mother insisted," she said. "She wants me to help her pickle something, or something. Mother's gone mad over putting things up." She stopped. Really, there was no need to explain so fully (and falsely). After all, she'd been here for hours.

"Okay," said Beatrice, gathering up the cards. "I'll walk you to the bus."

Betty said thank you and good-by to Mrs. Roman. She said good-by to Grandma and to Jack. She considered going to find the other children, who'd scattered, to say good-by to them, and decided it was unnecessary. She wasn't even sure they knew she'd been there.

"It was fun," she said to Beatrice, as they walked down the sad street toward the bus stop.

Beatrice gave her a curious look, and for a moment Betty thought she was going to say something honest and direct, such as "You didn't have fun, so why say you did?"

If she said something like that, Betty thought, I could explain how it is that I'm not used to a family like hers. I've been explaining it to myself all afternoon, but I'd sort of like to explain it to her. I could say that some of it *was* fun, that I'd like a chance to get used to them, that I know I wasn't very gracious, but I would like another chance.

Beatrice, after a moment, said, "It was nice to have you." She was very formal.

They continued down the street, Beatrice abstracted, Betty despondent. Well, she doubted if Beatrice would ask her again. It's my own fault, she said to herself. And, actually, I don't care.

The trouble was, she did care. But she didn't see what to do about it, except to offer an explanation that might only result in humiliation. Suppose she tried to explain and Beatrice said I don't know what you're talking about. Then where would she be? Better to let it go this way. No real unpleasantness had taken place, nothing for which apologies were in order. Something to explain, possibly, but since she didn't know how to make the explanation, let it be.

Fortunately the bus arrived almost as soon as they reached the corner. I could have walked here alone easily, Betty thought. It was nice of her to come with me. But they'd barely exchanged a word on the walk, so it hadn't helped. The good-bys were quick. Betty did not expect any mention of a further meeting, and there was none. Only her own hurried "Hope I'll see you soon," and Beatrice's "Yes, I hope so."

Feeling blue, she sat at a window seat and watched the drab streets change to nicer residential ones. Then they were on the highway, and presently going past the meadow and the orchard with the low stone wall. Betty rang the bell and got up, unbelievably happy to be getting home at last.

Elbows on the desk, chin on her hands, she read over her letter to Carol. All wrong. Too flip, too serious. Anyway, how did she know she'd been in love? If you were in love, you didn't get over it this quickly, did you? And all that nonsense about recognizing a diamond. They made simulated diamonds these days that only an expert could tell from the real thing. She was no expert in love, and so could have been fooled. And if she was over it, why talk about it?

The letter was, in fact, pointless. She tore it up.

"Dear Carol," she began on a fresh sheet. "Heaven knows I should be able to give you the outlines of life's drama here briefly enough. My cast of characters is so very very small. . . ."

7

FOR THE FIRST TIME IN HER life, she was experiencing the sense of exclusion. It was not unbearable. For one thing, she didn't quite believe it. Although it was happening, she had an underlying feeling that this was all a mistake, a package that had been delivered to the wrong address. Presently the phone would begin to ring, her day would bring easy frequent contacts with people who were important to her, as she to them. At any moment she would know, in all the ways she'd known it in Chicago, the security of being an unquestioned member of an unquestioned group. Not a group formed of rejects and remnants, not one of those with the faintly strained, faintly defiant expression so easily read as "I may not be much now, but just wait, I'll show them, one day I'll build the biggest bridge, be the biggest movie star, write the greatest book, I'll show them, these smug high-school kids who don't matter anyway." These fringe groups, these dejected defiers, had nothing to do with Betty Wilder. She remembered them from Chicago, remembered how, when she thought of or noticed them at all, she'd felt pity and distaste for them individually and collectively (and had observed but had no respect for their dreams-of-glory attitudes). There was no place for her in such a society.

Yet the phone did not ring, and in Norwood High School she was, as yet, important to no one. A so-so student, in large classes, she had not been particularly noticed. Most of her classmates knew her by name, greeted her, accepted her presence, and let it go at that. She could, without shyness or fear of being snubbed, take her place at nearly any table in the cafeteria, except those tacitly reserved by powerful cliques, the members of which seemed blind to her. There were no sororities in this high school, a fact which had at first (in her confidence) disappointed her, and now gave her a simply weakening sense of relief. To be so unable to find your place could at least be a matter of decent obscurity when there was no rush week to point it up.

Whenever she and Beatrice met, Beatrice was cordial. She introduced her to anyone who chanced to be standing by, and later that person would greet her also, and introduce her, and slowly she was getting to be known. But as for accepted . . .

What's the matter with them? she asked herself, more puzzled than alarmed. Is there something the matter with me? But I'm no different. I'm the same person I was in Chicago, where I had a nice safe place, and dates, and friends, and a security that enabled me to be kind to newcomers. Is *no one* here secure enough to take a risk on a stranger? But that, she realized, was silly. Always there were the safe, strong, entrenched people who could, with a nod, open doors that all your own battering could never budge. Betty was too wise to batter closed doors. She knew enough to wait until a possessor of the *Open Sesame* took the trouble to say it for her. Only, why did no one say it? Why had all this time gone by, only to find her still hovering, confused, at the portals?

A certain sense of justice, more developed in Betty than in many people her age, said that perhaps this was good for her. To know what it was to be excluded, to experience what some people had to know always, would make you a wiser, kinder person, would it not? Very well, she would examine and make the most of this chilling, unfamiliar experience. Only please, she said in an undirected prayer, please, let it not go on too long. I won't ever forget it, I'll remember and be kind in turn when once again I'm safe. Perhaps I wasn't always kind in the past. Perhaps in my security I only reached out to help people I knew my friends would accept, but after this . . . She turned away from the thought. Because it was not, she knew, an honest offer. Whoever it was she was propitiating would not believe her. Because, once enfolded, once accepted, she would do just as she had done before. Take a chance where there was not much risk. Extend a hand after making sure that the person could help herself.

We aren't very daring, she thought in a moment of scorn that almost made her strong. We're full of good intentions, if they don't get in our way, but we aren't courageous, or original, or really good. We play it safe.

There was just that moment of insight, and it passed, leaving her to circle once more around the bewildering question, what was wrong here in Norwood? Had it been merely because of seniority, because of the fact that she'd grown up with all the people, that she was so sure and certain in Chicago? That was not true. She'd been a member of the elite, the top, where, because they had no rivals, they could be friendlier than any other group. Carol had plucked Christine from almost certain disaster. A girl in a less confident group could not have done that, would not have attempted it. Carol could, because of where she stood. And I stood right beside her, Betty told herself now. We were the leaders. Nobody here would be taking such a risk with me. I can take care of myself, make my way, if just one person would say the first accepting word.

And her mother and father. They were so bewildered, so discreetly not showing it. They avoided mention of the telephone as if it were an unseemly word. They accepted her presence evening after evening as though it were a novelty and of course tomorrow she'd be off with her gang, and all this masquerade was conducted without a direct comment after the first couple of evenings.

"Staying home again tonight?" her father had said, that second day after his home-coming. "I rate, don't I?"

"You rate, Daddy, whether I stay home or not."

"Oh, sure, sure. It's just nice to have you show it so tangibly," he'd said with a grin.

On the third evening he'd said how fine it was, having the family all together this way. On the fourth they'd merely got along well together without mentioning it, and from then on there was no reference to the clearly deducible fact that for Betty there was no alternative.

One morning, when a couple of girls whose names—Ginny and Rowena—she knew, and whose place—at the summit—she knew, passed her in the hall and waved pleasantly, not slowing their steps, and called, "Hi, Betty, how are you?" not waiting for her reply, she stood rooted, looking after them. A girl named Eleanor, whose command was queenly in these halls, gave her a queenly nod and sailed by among her cohorts. The cohorts glanced quickly to see who'd been favored, but pressed on so as not to get out of the royal train.

Take a chance on me, Betty cried in her mind. You'd like me if you knew me. . . . Oh, please!

Then she shifted her books and walked on.

If only for Mother and Daddy's sake, she thought, I wish they'd look at me and realize that I'm really not an awful risk. Because if this keeps up, the three of us are going to be so embarrassed by what we're overlooking that we won't even have nice evenings together. And it had been sort of nice—this problem aside—being a family in a house this way. She supposed that people whose children were never popular must mind terribly. It was something she'd never given thought to until this week. What would it be like to know that your child, this person who meant so much to you, whose value you knew, was—for what reasons? through what unfairness? by what cruel turn of fate?—unacceptable in the eyes of his peers? Did you get used to it? After a while, after it had to be acknowledged, did it cease to trouble your days, disturb your dreams? Probably not. Probably you knew sorrow, a harsh, unsettled sorrow, most of the time. And you probably hoped always that it would change, that a new dress or a new tie or contact lenses or money or *something* would make life different for this person you loved and could not help.

She turned into her World History class, sat at her desk, and stared unseeing at a pink and blue map of Europe. They were learning, in this period, about people displaced, hungry, rootless, all over Europe. The result of war. She'd never stopped to think how people could be all those in spite of being fed, housed, protected. Unpopular, a square. So judged, you were rootless, hungry, without a place.

She did not believe in such a fate for herself. It was taking a little time, but she'd be all right. Only she, who had never expected it, never given it enough thought to wonder even briefly how it might be, was tasting the bitter brew of exclusion.

A little angrily, a little courageously, she said to herself, This is good for me.

The room had filled without her noticing it, and now Joe Preston, who had the desk next to hers, slid into place hurriedly, dropped a book that skidded over and hit her ankle.

"Whoops," he said. "Sorry. No damage done, I trust?"

"None," said Betty, turning to give him a direct glance and smile. George had said her smile would melt an ice cube at fifty paces. Not an inspired remark, but an inspiriting one to recall just now. She smiled at Joe Preston, with bright self-assurance, though he hadn't ever smiled at her, or appeared to notice her. He was the steady of that Ginny who'd passed her in the hall, he was a letter man, a VIP. Her smile was not the least bit forward, but it was the smile that had melted ice cubes for George, and George had been everything this boy was and more.

Joe, arranging his books, half returned her smile, then returned it fully. "How're you doing? Like it here?"

"It's very nice. The building, I mean," she said demurely. "Very pretty."

"Yeah. You should have seen what we labored through till they built this."

"No worse than Chicago, I imagine."

"That where you come from?" Belatedly, he seemed conscious of her first reply. "What do you mean, the building? Is that all you like about it here?" His glance coaxed her, and she wondered just how steady was his arrangement with Ginny. It was no part of her plan to antagonize Ginny.

Therefore she abandoned a perfectly easy approach—that of a pretty new girl being unaccountably ignored by girls who, you could indicate ever so gently but kindly, were perhaps jealous. She thought such a line would probably work with Joe Preston. He was not intimidatingly bright (she'd found that out in class) and he was conceited (you didn't have to find that out—his good-natured conceit shone out of his eyes in a candid manner). A boy like that was usually a pushover for a helpless girl who was being misused. Provided, of course, that she was pretty. Joe Preston might not have noticed her before, but now he considered her pretty and he intended her to know he did. So, with his slight underabundance of brains and overabundance of self-approval, he might very well fancy himself the powerful rescuer of a poor weak girl. It was her first line to the tower of the mighty, the first indication that someone might be persuaded to murmur the magic words that would crumble walls for her. But, because of Ginny, she had to be careful. Get off on the wrong foot there and she'd have all those girls down on her, and in that case she might as well take up embroidery or cross-country walking for the rest of her senior year. Boys might be kings, but it was the girls who ruled the court.

She shuffled helplessness quickly aside. Flirtatiousness,

of course, wouldn't do at all. She settled for an engaging semi-frankness. "Actually, I've hardly had a chance to get to *know* the place. I sort of get lost. And we're so busy getting settled in our house that I've hardly had a chance to get acquainted with people at all. I love living in a house. We always lived in an apartment."

This delight in something he took for granted charmed Joe, as she had intended it should. "But don't you know anybody yet?" he asked, with concern. Not to know anybody was clearly, and correctly, Betty realized now if she never had before, the worst thing that could befall a person.

"Only sort of. *You* know." She was friendly, not the least *bit* flirty. But she threw herself on his understanding.

"Oh, sure, I know," he said. The understanding was there. "Sure, it takes time."

"I know Beatrice Roman," she said tentatively. Did she? She didn't know her very well, but she could mend a fence, couldn't she? Go over to Perkins' Drugstore, stop Bea in the hall, initiate a conversation and keep it going. Wasn't it as much her fault as Beatrice's that their acquaintance was standing still, or moving backward? In this catch-as-catch-can society, this jungle known as high school, you had to make some moves, do something to help yourself. Waiting around remembering how popular you'd been in Chicago got you precisely nowhere.

"Bea?" he said approvingly. "She's a great kid. Works too hard, but a great kid."

Would working too hard exclude her from great kidship? Betty wondered, deciding Joe Preston was sort of a bore. Still, he was what she had to work with.

"Yes," she said. "She's awfully nice."

He knew Beatrice, and perhaps would report that Betty Wilder had spoken of her admiringly. Usually you like people who speak of you admiringly behind your back. It might lead Beatrice to overlook that discouraging afternoon's visit. Which was not, Betty added stubbornly, entirely my fault. She moved hastily away from that line of thinking. No matter where the fault lay, as the newcomer she had the most to gain from being once again in Beatrice's good graces.

"I like her family, too," she added deliberately, with truth. In retrospect, she did. They were so spirited, so very alive and real.

Without their noticing, Mr. Gorham, the history teacher, had achieved his desk and now rapped on it gently. "Class will begin," he said.

She, Joe, and the rest of the students gave him their varying degrees of attention.

When the period was over, Joe went up to Mr. Gorham's desk with a question, and Betty, lingering as long as she decently could, finally left the room. It was too bad, but to wait for him would be unthinkable. She'd see him again. He's my wedge, she told herself, yawning.

She considered going that very afternoon to Perkins' Drugstore to seek out Beatrice, but decided against it. It was usually mobbed with high-school people, and Beatrice, if she had time to notice her at all, would not have time to receive a proffer of friendship. By telephone, Betty decided. That's how I'll do it. I'll call her tonight and suggest that we do something on Sunday. I'll ask her to my house. Even if she can't, I'll be able to judge the temperature of her response.

I'll do what I can, she told herself, and decided not to worry about results.

Human beings are awfully sad, she thought in a moment of tenderness transcending her own considerations. Struggling so to keep our poor little egos afloat that we cannot, even if we wished to, notice when someone else's is being submerged. Poor, poor people.

At home she found her mother stretched out on a reclining chair in the back yard, toying with a whip from the willow tree, watching Cliff's Calvin munch his way across the meadow.

"Hi, darling," said Mrs. Wilder lazily. "Good day at school?"

Betty lay back in another chair, nodded vaguely, and said, "What have you done all day?"

"Not a thing," said her mother, frowning. "Not a

blessed thing. And I haven't done a thing for three full days. I feel like a terrible slacker, and I just can't seem to care."

"After all that laying up of provender, you're entitled to a rest."

"Well, perhaps. But why can't I be moderate? All work, or no work. I don't approve. Where do you suppose that middle road is that people talk about? Do you suppose anyone ever actually sets foot on it?"

"Darned if I know. Maybe it isn't there at all. Maybe it's something people have made up to add to our burdens."

"Darling," said Mrs. Wilder, with a quick change of mood, "do you feel burdened? I mean, is there anything troubling you that you could tell me?"

Betty moved uneasily. Don't pry, she beseeched her mother in silence. Don't probe into matters that I won't and can't share. You took care of your own problems when you were young, let me take care of mine. And if I can't take care of them, let me fail to in my own way.

"Nothing, Mother. Isn't Calvin looking well?"

"What? Oh, yes. Yes, he looks fine." There was a long pause, and then Mrs. Wilder straightened a little, relaxed again, and said, "Cliff rode him today."

"He did? When?"

"Early this afternoon. I looked out, and there was Cliff, tying a saddle—or whatever you do with a saddle—to Calvin's back. Then he got on, just like a cowboy, and rode off. He looked very handsome."

He looks handsome with or without a horse, Betty thought, and then reminded herself that Clifton's looks were no concern of hers. "Well, that must have been fun," she said idly. "For both of them."

"I wonder if the horse does think it's fun. No way of telling with animals, of course."

"No." She wished she could have seen Clifton on the horse. Not for any particular reason, just because . . . well, just because she wished she could have.

"I guess he's awfully busy," Mrs. Wilder said. "Cliff, I mean. Calvin doesn't appear to be overworked."

Betty's heart warmed toward her mother, and this rather sweet oblique explanation for the fact that Clifton Banks was showing no interest in her. But again she did not want to reply, nor get into any sort of conversation that might touch upon her present lonely situation. "Did you get those bulbs?" she asked.

"I got them," Mrs. Wilder said slowly. "Yes, I got tulips and paper white narcissus and crocuses and daffodils and hyacinths. . . ." Her voice picked up. "It's going to be beautiful in the spring. Really, I do love living in a house, don't you?"

"Yes," Betty said. "I do."

She wanted to be back in Chicago, in the apartment she knew, going to the unsightly school where she was safe and popular. She wished she'd never heard of Norwood, N. Y., had never seen this house, didn't ever have to know how beautiful it would be in spring with all the flowers coming up. What will be happening to me in the spring? It's all very well for Mother and Daddy, and all these bulbs that will know their place and keep it so handsomely. What about me?

But she looked at her mother's bright face, at the little lines edging her eyes, at the unmade-up, softly curving mouth. "Since this is the week end, suppose I help you plant all these crocuses and hyacinths and daffodils and what not?" she said.

The fact that you had to keep your own ego afloat did not require you to push somebody else's under. And it was nice to see her mother looking so happy at the prospect of planting bulbs that would be flowers next spring.

8

ON SUNDAY AFTERNOON, AS she had nothing else to do, Betty went for a walk. She crossed the highway, climbed over the orchard wall, went down across the orchard to a field beyond, and wandered idly there till she found a little brook with a wooden bridge crossing it. The planks of the bridge were warm, and she sat there, dangling her legs.

The water was not very clear, not very lively, but to Betty any brook at all was enchantment. She discerned a few small fish cruising around down there, and now and then a frog startled her by leaping from the tall stiff grass to disappear with a splash that barely wrinkled the indolent surface of the water. The sun was hot and low, an Indian-summer sun that gave her a sense of fondness and loss, as leavetakings do, and the air's warmth was musky, like peach fluff, and a little sharp, like pepper.

She put her arms on the lower railing, rested her cheek on the back of one hand, swung her legs lazily and wondered if it were possible to think about nothing. Could you say to your mind, Rest now and don't do anything? For a while I'll just feel things, just be aware of the sun's heat and the smell of this little brook and the sight of leaves flying in flocks to the ground. Could you do that? She could not. Her body was aware of the sights and the sounds and the smells of the afternoon, but even as she looked at that young tree and studied its old leaves, curled and browning, her mind recalled Beatrice Roman's voice on the phone, and her mind had no intention of taking a rest. It wanted to remember, and remember it did.

People call their souls their own, she thought. But I've never heard anyone say, My mind's my own. I have a mind to, I've made up my mind, I won't change my mind. But never, My mind's my own.

"Betty?" Beatrice had said. "Oh, sure, Betty. How are you? Getting along all right, I hope."

"I'm getting along fine. I am just wondering, though . . . are you busy tomorrow?"

Beatrice laughed. "Ask me something reasonable. I'm always busy."

"Oh."

Should she read that as dismissal? Not necessarily. It could be just comment. Beatrice sounded perfectly friendly. Besides, Betty reminded herself, you said you'd take some trouble, so don't go sulking off just because the girl doesn't spring at you with suggestions. This is your problem, not hers. You handle it.

"Well, what I was really wondering, Bea, was whether you'd come over here tomorrow for a while. We could sit in the back yard and have tea and talk. That is, if you have time."

"Gosh, Betty, I honestly don't think I have. You know what it's like around here on Sunday."

That sounded nice. Sort of intimate, as though she were familiar with the details of the Roman household.

She was familiar enough with their Sundays to realize that Beatrice undoubtedly spoke the truth when she said she didn't have time.

And yet . . . wasn't she going to say that perhaps Betty could come over there? Or, failing that, say something about a meeting in the near future? It seemed that she was not. They had an amicable discussion. Betty asked after various members of the Roman family, asked after the pets. Beatrice inquired for her parents, and they came to the end of that conversational rope. There being nothing then left to hang on to, Betty said good-by and hung up. Her father and mother were outside, so no one was aware of this attempt of hers. That should be a comfort, she said to herself. All right, it's a comfort. Good. Now what?

Well, now was no different from ten minutes ago, when she had not yet telephoned. The day was the same, the hour but slightly advanced, and Beatrice had not been unfriendly. It will just take time, Betty assured herself. It's only a matter of time.

She ignored a bitter little ball of hurt and anger that had formed in her stomach. She had no right to be hurt, and anger would be disastrous. Anger, as she knew from a few examples of pained, furious girls in Chicago, opened no doors. That . . . what was her name? she couldn't remember . . . a great square girl without charm, who'd tried unsuccessfully to attach herself to their group, and had then lashed out in the gym locker room one day, "Who do you think you are, you bunch of jerks? Why, I'd be ashamed to be caught dead with you, you bunch of . . ." And she'd employed a couple of words that they all knew but certainly never used. Carol, Christine, Betty and a group of assorted onlookers had turned away in embarrassment. We weren't outraged, she recalled now. We were disgusted, and a little afraid of her, the way you'd be of an unknown excited animal. We didn't want, deliberately, to hurt her. We just wanted nothing to do with her. The unkindest hurt of all.

Betty under no circumstances would ever allow herself to be that angry. Never would she be angry or hurt enough to betray herself in such a way. I'd go without a word from a fellow being all my life before I'd create such a picture for people to remember. Yet she knew that even on a milder scale anger was no weapon, except against yourself. So you could not be angry, you could not be hurt. These were hazardous luxuries. You just had to wait, and understand that these things took time.

I'm certainly learning patience the hard way, she told herself ruefully, and then thought that no doubt it was never learned in any other.

She looked in the hall mirror and let it tell her that she looked very nice in her red plaid walking shorts and pink shirt. She gave a wry smile that didn't fool the mirror and didn't fool her, and went out to the back yard.

Her father was stretched out on the grass, a book beside him, hands beneath his head, eyes squinting at the sky. He cocked a brow at her approach and said, "Come to labor, or to watch? I'm beat. Beat, I tell you. Beat, beat, beat . . ."

"He put in two tulip bulbs and picked up a cigarette he'd dropped," said Mrs. Wilder.

"Poor Daddy," said Betty. "That must have been exhausting."

"Women make fun of me," Mr. Wilder said thoughtfully. "I don't know why it is, but the fact remains that women make fun of me. Make what you will of it."

"Because you're funny," said Betty, smiling at him.

"It's a side of myself I never see." He sat up. "What's on your program?"

"Nothing much."

Her father and mother avoided each other's eyes, and Betty pretended she didn't notice. We won't be able to keep this up, she thought. We'll reach a point where their discretion will just be tactlessness, where we'll have to say something because it will be too awkward to go on saying nothing. But not yet. Still for a little while they could pretend that there was nothing on their minds more pressing than the flower bulbs and whether squirrels ate them.

"I hear they do," said Mr. Wilder gravely. "I hear their depredations are not to be believed. I hear they come like barbarian hordes to lay waste your garden and gnaw the fruit of your labors."

"It'll be my labors they're gnawing," said Mrs. Wilder as she dug. "Betty offers assistance and you offer advice, but *I* labor."

"Gee, that's right," Betty said. "I did say I'd help you." She looked around. "Where's a trowel or something?"

Mrs. Wilder shook her head. "You're too late, dear. I just buried the last hyacinth. Now it's up to heaven."

"And the squirrels, of course," said her husband.

"Stop dwelling on those squirrels, will you?" she said, with the faintest edge in her voice.

She isn't annoyed with Daddy, Betty thought. She's upset about me, and it comes out in other ways because she can't say anything. Briefly, she wondered if it would be kinder to come right out and say, I know what you're thinking and I know you're upset, and if it will help you any, go ahead and talk about it. If it'll make you feel better, give me sympathy or advice, whatever you want.

Only she couldn't.

She sat on the grass beside her father and picked up his book. "What are you reading—history again?"

"I may learn something. But I'm not sure, you know, that books are the answer to everything. I used to think so. And then I decided one day that you can't learn everything from books, and from there it was just a step to deciding you can't learn anything from them."

"Then what happened?"

"Why, after a while I decided you can't learn anything from living, either, so I'm back to books. I've been trudging around *that* circle for years, learning nothing except the names of the kings and queens of England, which are very handy for saying in your mind when you can't sleep."

"It isn't true," Betty muttered, "so I don't see why you say it."

"Egbert, a sort of protégé of Charlemagne's, established himself as the first King of England in 828 A.D. After that—"

"It isn't true," Betty said loudly, "that you've learned nothing."

"Comparatively little. Which in its way is learning, of course. I'm reminded of Gertrude Stein, who on her deathbed said, 'I know the answer, but what is the question?'"

When her father spoke this way, she never knew whether it was in order to hear himself and meant little or nothing to her, or whether he had some purpose that she was too dull to grasp. Most of the time, she made no effort to find out.

But today, sitting on the warm planks of the wooden bridge above the little brook, she recalled his words. Was he trying to tell her that the answer didn't matter, the question was all? If you didn't know the question, it wouldn't make much difference whether the answer was or wasn't important. Did he mean that the point was not learning, but trying to learn? Was that supposed to be an answer to a question which, like life itself, you couldn't possibly comprehend? I'm making it too complicated, she told herself. In an indirect way, he was telling me, reminding me, that everybody's trying and everybody's confused. Which I already knew.

Parents always think they can help you, and certainly it's nice of them to try, but to my way of thinking we'd all be better off if a proclamation were issued saying that you can no more help another person by telling what you feel than you can make him hear a piece of music by telling him what it sounds like to you. Experience should come marked like a commuter's ticket—nontransferable.

A flock of crows flew raggedly overhead, an ant carried something too big for him across the flooring of the bridge, a frog sprang from stone to brook, sending the little fish flashing away, and Clifton Banks came across the meadow carrying a gun.

She saw him when he was quite a distance off, and her heart began to pump thickly, her limbs were seized with a sudden uneasy languor, so that she could not, if she'd wanted to, scramble up and start away. Passionately still, she waited, knowing he might turn aside and be gone long before she had the courage to lift her eyes from the brook where the little fish were gadding.

She waited, not looking, troubled with the heavy beating of her heart.

And then his step was on the wooden bridge, halting, and he stood looking down at her, the gun with its stock broken hanging beside him. Betty turned her head, lifted her eyes, and sighed. "Hello," she said, and added nothing.

"Hello."

A moment passed and she heard, more distinctly than she'd heard before, the stir of dried grass, the caw of crows, the shush shush shush of water running lazily around stones and away.

I will not speak, she thought. Anything that's said will be said by him, or he can just take his gun and keep walking. He's caused me enough trouble already. Unconcernedly, she dropped a pebble into the brook and watched the ripples rise and widen. Concentrate on all those things they say about ripples. She concentrated, but could not recall anything that had been said about ripples. Still, one way and another, there was a good deal of talk about them. . . .

"May I sit down?" he said.

"Please do."

The bridge is free, the brook and the meadow are free. And so, for that matter, am I. Free of anything, and, most of all, free of you, though I don't suppose you're interested, or would be interested to know that for a little while I loved you. I loved your truck, your horse, your prickly, unforthcoming mother, and everything that pertained to you. It was like nothing I've ever felt before, but it's all over now.

"What are you shooting at?" she said.

"Crows."

"I didn't hear your gun."

"Haven't shot it yet."

"Oh."

He laid the gun beside him with care, and the barrel gleamed dully in the sun. "Nice day," he said.

"Lovely."

"I didn't feel like working."

"That's unusual."

"Not really. Lots of times I don't. But I have to."

He spoke matter-of-factly, but she softened toward him, remembering how, at the stand one day, Mrs. Banks had said, "Sure, Clifton's been working all his life. So have I. So have lots of people." She thought now of Clifton as a little boy. He would have been a handsome little boy, and he would have gone seriously about his work, knowing it had to be done. A little like Jack Roman? she wondered. Sober, but with Sinbad dreams of finding jewels, of reaping rewards?

"When you were a little boy, did you ever think you might find valuable things that people had lost?"

Cliff laughed. "Like Jack, you mean? He's sure determined. Says all this stuff gets left in taxis, in buses, in trains, on the sidewalk, so why in heck doesn't he find it? I think that kid thinks half the world is losing diamonds every day and it's just sheer bad luck he hasn't been in the right place at the right time. I'll give him this, he's a great one for hanging onto an idea."

"That's more hanging onto a dream, isn't it?"

"Perhaps you're right. Funny sort of dream, though. So practical. Modern."

"We have to move with the times."

He grinned, turning his face toward her, so that she was compelled to turn to him. For a moment they looked into each other's eyes, while his smile faded and another expression came. A rather wondering look that he bent on her raptly for a moment before he turned away in silence.

He hasn't bothered much with girls, she realized suddenly. He's too awkward and surprised to be used to this sort of thing. Elation flickered and leaped within her, bright and abrupt as a struck match. He was shy, and he'd been too busy to notice girls. His mother, in fact, had said that (perhaps purposefully) to her mother, who had duly reported it, but that had been when Betty hadn't wanted to talk about him, hadn't wanted to remember him at all. She remembered it now, and believed it. There had been something so untried, so perplexed, in his expression just now. He'd been noticing her and hadn't even known how to disguise it.

All her own feelings came back in a generous way,

mingled with tenderness. She felt she knew so much more than he did.

And so much, she thought in a quickly shuttered moment of clarity, for my independence, my indifference to him, my knowledge that he's not my kind of person and I'm not his and so that would be that. It took one look for me to waver, and in another minute I'm going to forget I ever thought such things.

He asked me for a date once, she reminded herself. He'd hardly met me, but he asked me for a date. Not as if he were anxious, almost as if the words were being dragged from him. Which, in its way, is better. She thought—tentatively, not wanting to build too much on it, for fear that again he would elude her, for some reason notice and then leave her—that he had been drawn to her from the very beginning as she had to him. Not so ardently, that was clear. He had not taken one look and known that he would remember this moment always, and he had not spent weeks watching her driveway, her window, for a glimpse of her. But notice her he had, and he hadn't got over it, no matter if he disapproved of her behavior at the Romans'. It was one thing to stay away, as he'd been doing, but another to turn and meet her eyes, as he just had.

Her spirits lifted, airy and giddy. But carefully, doing nothing to alarm him, she spoke of indifferent things. She told him about the bulbs they were planting, and he said it was true that squirrels were the enemy to keep your eye on. He inquired after the dishwasher, and she assured him that it was doing well. "In the best of health," she said.

They were silent again. A frog leaped, his legs trailing like two spokes of a fan. "I never knew before that frogs were knock-kneed," she said, her voice so idle, so bemused that the shyest boy could feel no threat.

"They are, aren't they?" He gave her an appreciative glance. "I'd never see a thing like that."

She felt so pleased she wanted to laugh. "I just happened to notice." If he'd been George, she'd have added, It's nothing, really, don't give me too much credit. But love for Clifton reduced her to sitting, her hands on the rail faintly shaking, feeling wildly silently happy that she'd observed that frogs were knock-kneed. There seemed to be a possibility that love removed your sense of humor, but in her state of mind she thought it would be all right if she never had a good laugh again. Love was serious and sympathetic. She decided that laughter might be out of place.

But I wonder . . . I wonder . . . Will he love me?

She dropped another pebble into the brook and watched the ripples and had no thoughts about them. She thought, If I am gentle and wise about this, if I become what he wants a girl to be (which is what? Well, familyish rather than frivolous was the nearest she could come to what she felt Clifton wanted a girl to be), then will he love me?

The silence began to prolong itself too much. "Yes," she said reflectively, turning again to the subject of the bulbs. "Mother and I had a wonderful time putting them in." She'd handed her mother a trowel and gone for a walk. Still, no need for Cliff to know that. "We can hardly wait for spring. We've never had a garden before." There was a genuinely wistful note in her voice. In Chicago she'd never wanted a garden, never thought about a garden. But she was looking forward to one now, almost as much as her mother was. "We had geraniums, and ivy. But that's not the same." Was she overdoing it? Apparently not. He was looking at her as you'd look at an underprivileged child who is unconsciously betraying the poverty of his life. She gave him a sad little look, sighed faintly, and ran her finger along the weathered railing.

She wasn't, entirely, making up a picture for him. Until a little while ago she *had* felt wistful and lonely and sad. And before she could simply give way and be happy, she had the part about the Romans to get through, and for that the picture she was painting was necessary.

Unexpectedly, he helped her out. "Funny," he said, "but I really did get you all wrong."

"Wrong? Wrong when?"

"Oh, you know. That day at the Romans'."

She smiled softly. "They're so nice, aren't they?"

Looking a little vexed, he nodded. "Sure. They're swell. Only I didn't—"

"Didn't what?" she said with gentle encouragement.

"Well," he burst out, "I didn't think you knew it."

"I see," she sighed. "Well, they felt the same way, I suppose. I've never been around such a big family, and I was confused and didn't talk much, I guess. But I liked them, really."

"We certainly did get you wrong."

We? she thought. They'd talked her over, then. Probably not in laudatory terms, but at least they'd remembered she existed.

"Betty—" he began, and did not know how to go on. That's all right, she told him silently, lovingly. Just say Betty, just say my name over and over, because the rest doesn't matter. It will straighten itself out.

"It's all right," she said. "I can understand that I must have seemed—standoffish. I'm not even getting along well in school," she said, forgetting the somewhat spuriously pitiful role to concentrate on what was real. "I can't quite understand it, because I was popular enough at home. In Chicago, I mean. But here . . ." She lifted her shoulders, let them slump a little. "Maybe I've seemed standoffish in school, too. I don't know. I've decided to take everything one day at a time. I was thinking just a little while ago that it really wouldn't matter if for one more day nobody talked to me. I could always take it for one more day. So I'll take it one more day at a time, and after a while it'll be all right. Does that make sense?"

She'd been speaking seriously, but his glance made her feel so pleasantly brave and ill-used that she slipped back into the underprivileged-child role, scarcely noticing. She lifted questioning eyes to his, and *saw* him begin to fall in love. Like that, she thought, just like that.

I love you, Cliff, she told him silently, and meant to, and knew she did.

I guess I love you, too, he said, not meaning to, not knowing that he did.

With a nervous gesture, he patted his gun.

"Tell me about your work," she said quickly, to calm him, to claim his interest in an unpossessive way. She remembered, long ago, saying to George (to claim *his* interest), "Tell me about entomology. What *is* it?" A year later he'd still been explaining. "I mean," she said "I'm never quite sure what you do, except everything."

He smiled a little. "What I want is to be a builder one day. I'm sort of hoping to get apprenticed to someone good, like Mr. Perone."

"Apprenticed?" she said, caught by the medieval sound of the word.

"You serve a four-year apprenticeship before you can get your journeyman's card."

What marvelous words, she thought, but didn't say so. He might think it was condescending, though she wouldn't mean it to be. "What do you do in the four years?"

"Learn the trade. From the ground up. Or even from under the ground up. They usually put you to digging ditches at first. You work up to roof rafters," he said, with his elusive smile. "I mean, you wouldn't expect a first-year apprentice to cut roof rafters, but you'd ask and expect a third-year apprentice to do it and do it right. And you learn to read blueprints. I've been teaching myself to do that, because a builder might omit stuff or only teach subjects as they came up in everyday work. I want to know how to read them right. And you learn to tell properly seasoned wood. That is, if the builder himself knows, and I wouldn't work for anyone who didn't. . . ."

It's really just like George, she thought, listening with interest. She always liked to hear people talk on subjects they knew and liked. Cliff discoursed happily for a while, but at length he sighed, squinted at the sun, and said, "This has been great. But I have to get back. I have a load of bricks to take across county."

He got to his feet, extended a hand to her, and she took it, leaped up lightly, close to him. They stood, hands clasped, looking at each other for a long time. Then, slowly, not shyly or boyishly but with a great deal of tenderness, he drew her into his arms and kissed her.

When they moved apart, he said in a warm rough voice that was filled with wonder, "I'm in love with you. Do you know that? I've fallen in love with you."

"I know, Cliff. I know. I'm in love with you, too."

"Are you?" he said somberly. He looked so bewildered that she wanted to hug him and say, Darling, it's all right, don't be afraid, it's really, truly all right.

"I am, Cliff. I fell in love with you that first day you came to the house."

He groaned a little and pulled her back in his arms. "Look," he said, after he'd kissed her again. "Sit down here a minute. I'm . . . mixed up."

Obediently she sat with him, and waited for him to speak.

He put his head on his doubled fists, leaning on the railing, and said, not looking at her, "I'll tell you something funny. But you're not to laugh."

"I won't laugh."

"I've never kissed a girl before."

She believed him. He was nineteen, and handsome, and girls would have been wanting his attentions, his kiss, for years. But she believed him. And she thought with overwhelming sadness of George, of Matthew, of Weldon. *Oh, never to have known them.* To be able to say, clearly and truly, I have never been kissed but by you, my love, my darling. They didn't count, they were nothing, she never had loved them, not even George. But she couldn't say to Cliff, I have never been kissed before.

"Cliff—"

He put his hand, warm and firm, on hers. "Don't say anything, Betty. You're a beautiful, lovely girl, and of course guys have been in love with you."

"But that's one thing I can say," she cried. "I have never never been in love with anyone but you, Cliff. Not ever, not even a little bit." Forgive me, George, she thought. I did love you in a way, but not like this, and I have to be able to tell him that he's the only one I ever loved.

"You must think I'm sort of unrealistic," he said, still enfolding her hand. "I know a girl like you would have been kissed before. Myself—I guess I've just been too darn busy. I really figured that girls—I mean getting involved with them—was just a stupid waste of time. Maybe," he said, after a long pause, "I was waiting for you."

"I was, for you. I had to wait for you, to be in love. Cliff, darling, I do love you so." She gazed ecstatically down the course of the brook. "I never have called anybody darling before. I never could have."

"I like it." He turned her hand over and studied it. "Do you remember that day in the drugstore when I asked you for a date?"

"Of course I do. I remember everything."

"It sort of surprised me, asking you."

"I knew."

"Did you? Funny . . . I was just talking to you, and suddenly I thought, I'd like to see her again. Soon."

"And then . . . the Romans," she sighed.

"Don't think about it, Betty. It's all right now."

"Yes, now it's all right."

They grew silent, consumed with each other's presence, and curiously tired. The sun moved lower. Cliff turned and looked at her lingeringly, almost studiously, as if she were something to be learned. "I really have to get back," he said. "Betty?"

"Darling . . . yes?"

"Do you want to go with me while I deliver the bricks?"

She burst out laughing. She was wildly happy to laugh this way, indefinably relieved at the change his question made in the air between them. She threw her arms around his neck and said, "I will deliver the bricks with you to the ends of the earth."

"Well, just across county will do," he said. He caught her tight for a moment, released her, picked up his gun and said, "I don't understand a thing that's happened, but it's the most wonderful feeling I've ever had."

All that I have wanted, Betty thought, all that I could want, or ever will want, is here beside me in this boy— this man. Humble with love, she asked herself the old question . . . How have I been so lucky, why am I so blessed?

9

THAT LAST YEAR OF HIGH
school never was like the years of school in Chicago.
The time came when she sat with Ginny and Rowena
at lunch, walked with Eleanor to the bus when school
was out, chatted easily with Joe Preston and boys like
that in the lab, on the campus, on the streets downtown.
They had been, as she'd thought, looking her over, taking their comfortable cruel time about it, but she could
have become one of them finally. They made the over-
tures she'd hoped for, seemed bewildered when she
gently, without explaining, put them off. They remained friendly and solicitous, considering her something of a mystery.

She did not, any longer, wish to be a power in the
school.

School was just something to fill up the day, because

Clifton would be working anyway, and because, even though they wanted it, though they would have loved nothing more, they could not be together all the time. Their parents, their society, their own upbringing told them that a girl of seventeen and a boy of nineteen could not be in each other's company as much as she and Cliff wished to be. That would have been every minute of the day and night, and certainly parents, society and upbringing could not accept that.

"I miss you so," she'd tell him, riding to school in his truck in the morning. "I miss you so that it frightens me. All day I go around, doing things and talking to people and taking notes and acting as if I were alive, and I'm never alive until I'm with you again."

"Well, I'm the same," he'd sigh. He was never as articulate as she was, not so desperate to put felt things into words. He did not say I love you nearly as often, as irrepressibly as she did. Yet, when she'd long to hear the words, she would know in some other, surer, older part of her mind that he told her all the time.

He told her even in his way of understanding things that she despised in herself. She wanted that time with him in the morning, wanted to have him stop in that beloved, time-buffeted truck and wait at her gate till she rushed out with her books and her joy at the sight of his face. And yet, reluctantly, hitting at herself for the ugliness of mind it seemed to imply, she did not want him to drive her right to the school, did not want to arrive in the truck that she adored the sight of.

He had said, that Sunday as they drove across county with the load of bricks, "Let me drive you in the morning, Betty. I can stop and take you to school."

"Won't it make you late? Can you fit it in?"

"I can fit it in. I'll always get my work done, and it would be a little extra time. I don't have an awful lot."

Breathless at each admission that he wanted to be with her, she nodded with happiness. But then in the morning, as they approached the high school, she knew with a failing heart that she did not want to arrive in this manner before the general student gaze. She did not want Ginny or Rowena or Eleanor to see her climb down from this workingman's vehicle. It isn't Cliff, she told herself with anguish. It's this truck. It's so used, such a thing of labor, so—but she would not, even in her mind, say lower-class—it's so banged up. If he had a car—

"You can let me out here," she'd said quickly. "I don't mind the extra couple of blocks, and it will save you turning around." Don't know what I'm saying, darling, she pleaded. Don't *know* what a snob, what a vulgarian I am. Because it was vulgar, it was boorish and lacking in any kind of taste or simplicity, to feel this way. And she couldn't help it. Only, don't you know, she prayed, and met his eyes, and knew he did know.

"That'll be fine," he said gently. "I can go right on, this way."

"*Cliff*—"

"I love you, Betty. Any way you are, I love you."

She walked the two blocks to school feeling sick. I don't deserve him. He didn't finish high school, his mother keeps a fruit stand, he drives an old laborer's truck, and he has more breeding than anyone else I've ever known. Yes, Clifton had breeding. She had only airs.

She went through the day in misery.

She took the bus home. There'd been nothing said about meeting her after school, but that, of course, was because he would be working and really couldn't fit her in. She had come into the house and begun to wait, to wait for the sight of the spurned truck in the Banks driveway. Two hours would have to go by at least, and she doubted if she could get through two hours. How am I going to wait until then? What am I going to do with two hours, or maybe three? How can I stand it until I see him and explain?

She changed her clothes and sat at her desk, trying to study. But words moved around the pages of her books like bits of glass in a kaleidoscope. And her mind, too, was jagged and tumbled like a kaleidoscope, so that every time she thought she got the picture it shifted and some new unrecognizable pattern was flung before her vision.

He said he loved me any way I am, so can't I accept that and know that he'll be forbearing with faults in myself that I hate but can't help? I can give him so much. My heart, my thoughts, my whole life's being, so can't he take and understand some few faults in me? Wouldn't all that she could give be enough, balance what she could not? It was a picture, a pattern of sorts, but it shifted as though a hand had reached out to turn the kaleidoscope even as she looked, and she asked herself scornfully what sort of love would propose how much was enough.

She left the desk, wandered around the room, lay down on her bed without removing the spread, and gave herself up to repine. *I'm not worthy. I don't deserve to be in love with him, because my spirit is so small. My heart, I think, is capable of love, but a heart alone won't do. I have a niggling little spirit that creates barriers of shame where no shame should be. Oh, but, Cliff, Cliff, Cliff . . . I do love you so.*

And would he, after all, come back?

This new fear sent her to her feet again, and she went to the window to stare with a burning need at his empty driveway. He'd said he loved her. He had understood. But he could love and understand and still not find forgivable what had really been an unforgivable action, one that had betrayed all the poverty of her values. Suddenly she was sure he would never come to her again. *I had a chance*, she told herself. *The most beautiful chance of my life. And this thing that I term my pride has lost it for me.*

But words were no help. Stringing them out and adding to them, no help. . . .

Nothing is going to help, she thought tiredly. *Only to see Cliff again, to be with him, in his arms. Only to hear him say again, I love you.*

It would be hours before he came home. *If he came home . . . and did not call, did not come to her? Then I'll just have to go to him*, she realized. *I used to think it was shocking or funny when a girl said she couldn't live without some boy. But I know now what they meant. Because I cannot endure, or cope, or be, if I don't have Cliff.*

Only fifteen minutes had passed.

I love that truck, she thought. *And I'm ashamed of it.*

Is that how I feel about Cliff, too? But she couldn't bear this thought in her mind. She turned it out quickly, with horror, and decided to do something—anything at all—to keep from thinking any more.

She went to the bureau and put on fresh make-up, almost without looking, just to be sure her appearance would not alarm her mother, and went downstairs to see if she could help with something. Which, she thought dryly, will alarm her more.

"Mother, where are you?"

"In the basement, dear. I'm counting how many jars of things. It's *wonderful.*" Mrs. Wilder came upstairs, humming. She wore jeans and an old shirt of her husband's. Betty, who disapproved of women dressing like girls (though not of girls dressing like boys), began to scowl, quickly changed her mind. What if her mother did dress in ways she did not like? How many things did she do that her mother didn't like? And she's slim, Betty thought. She doesn't look actually ridiculous. Why not let her alone? Why do I always want to carp? I said, and it wasn't so very long ago, that if I loved Cliff, I would try to be the sort of girl he liked. Well, his mother dresses like a lumberjack, but he never seems to mind. Why don't I do likewise?

"I wondered if there was anything I could do."

Mrs. Wilder did not look surprised or ask if she were ill, for which Betty was glad. Mother has grace, she thought. And, much of the time, so has Daddy. Which leaves me all by myself, all by myself in a corner. She gave her Mother a pale smile and said, "Well, how about it?"

"Oh, there's no end of stuff to do. Would you want to vacuum the living room for me? I've been meaning to for three or four days, but somehow I always get lured into the kitchen or out in the garden. For all I know, there may be bats in there by now, but it seems a pity to waste such weather harnessed to a vacuum. But if you would . . ."

"Be glad to."

She was, in fact, glad to be given a task that was noisy, because she did not feel like talking. Her throat ached, and she moved in a soft, thick atmosphere that would make any communication difficult. And revealing. Her mother had this uncanny, frequently unwelcome ability to detect moods, and could not always be relied on to keep silence. Probably because she loves me, Betty thought, getting out the vacuum and dragging it into the living room. Her mother's love, right now, could not reach or solace her.

The vacuum roared in her ears, and Mrs. Wilder had to call twice. "Betty! . . . Betty!"

She heard, flicked the vacuum off, and turned, trying not to look irritable.

"Phone, darling."

"Oh. Thanks."

Who, who, who? It would be Beatrice. It would be a delegation composed of Rowena, Ginny and Eleanor or any of those people she'd have died of joy to hear from yesterday morning or any of the days before. It would be Hollywood saying they wanted her to star in everything from now on, or the President saying he'd decided to resign in her favor. It would be anyone in the world except it would not be Cliff. Not the only voice she ever wanted to hear . . .

"Hello?" she said faintly.

"Betty?"

She closed her eyes and wanted to sink to the floor with joy, with weakness, with relief. Darling, darling, she crooned at the phone, and, because her mother was in the kitchen, said, "Why, hello, Cliff . . . hello."

"Betty," Mrs. Wilder called, "I'm going down in the cellar again." The cellar door closed, and Betty took one fleeting moment to wonder how she could ever think or say a thing against her mother before she turned again to her love. "Cliff . . . where are you?" Her voice was husky and caressing, the ache gone from her throat, the fear and pain gone as if they hadn't been.

He laughed a little. "I'm on the job. I just took off for a minute, because I knew you'd be home, and I wanted to say I love you, and I didn't want to wait until tonight."

"I love you, Cliff. Do you know how much I love you?"

"I don't think I do. Do I?"

"Try to, darling. Please."

"All right. But you keep telling me, so I don't forget." He sounded joyous and confident. No hint of hurt or reproach was in his voice. Only love and the pleasure of talking to her, of calling her unexpectedly and so giving her pleasure.

Was I wrong? she wondered. Maybe he didn't guess. Oh, if he didn't, I'll never be so base again. I'll get out of his truck in the dead center of the school buildings as if it were a coach and four.

"Cliff, when will you be home? I watch for your truck. Have I told you how I watch for your truck every night, and look at the light in your window and think about you and wonder what you're doing?"

"You haven't told me plenty of things," he said. "There hasn't been time."

"But there will be," she said.

"Yes," he said, quietly now. "Yes, there'll be all the time in the world, for us. Betty, I have to get back. See you tonight."

"Cliff—"

"Yes?"

"You didn't tell me when you'd be home."

"You look for the truck," he said gaily. "I like that idea, having you watch for me. Good-by."

He was gone, and Betty, transfigured with happiness, returned to the vacuum.

Yet in the days and weeks that followed, he never did drive her right to the school entrance. He made no reference to it, but dropped her at the same corner each morning. In the beginning, when she'd looked as if she might protest, he'd smiled, reaching across her to open the truck door.

"I can go straight on," he said. "Saves turning around." As if she had never said the words, as if it were his own idea.

Betty, who didn't read much, tried to remember a poem about the worm in the bud. That's what this action of hers might prove to be. A concealed thing, eating secretly at their love. But she wondered why *he* never said anything, never indicated that he knew what was implied in that two-block walk she took from the truck each morning. Were they afraid to know what it meant? Afraid, then, really to know each other?

In time, she put this thought away. Perhaps she was wrong, perhaps she exaggerated. She would not think of it. She would ignore it out of existence, love it out of existence, make it nothing. She walked the two blocks because it was more convenient, to get a little exercise, so that Cliff wouldn't have to turn around.

And school was something that occupied her day until she could see him again.

Apart from casual daily contacts, she saw nothing of her fellow students, with the exception of Beatrice Roman, who (she would always be sure at Clifton's prompting) came around to her locker one afternoon shortly after that Sunday.

"Hi, Betty," she said, as if the meeting were chance. As if, too, there had been no interval of distance between them. "How have you been? How are your classes?"

Betty shrugged a little. She did well enough in school. But never, except perhaps in that Latin class with Miss Rory, had she felt any ardor for learning. Her father, who knew this and deplored it, had a way of saying that it would be different when she got to college.

"A girl with a mind like yours simply must respond sometime," he'd say, whether to reassure her or himself she did not know.

She assumed she'd go to college, but never wondered why she assumed it, nor asked herself why she wanted to go. It was just sort of taken for granted, and she'd applied to three schools. One of them would take her, and next year she'd be a college student, but when anyone asked about her classes, she tended to give that lift of the shoulders.

"They're all right," she said. "Can't say more than that. Either I don't bring out the best in teachers, or they don't bring out the best in me. How are yours?"

They had started for the door together without consulting each other, and Betty thought, I'll walk to Perkins' with her, and sometime in the walk I'll ask, once again, if she's busy on Sunday. If she says she's busy this time, I'll just have to give up.

Cloaked in Clifton's love, she felt safe, able to take any rebuff, if rebuff there had to be. Besides, she wasn't sure now she wanted Beatrice to come over on Sunday. Maybe Cliff wouldn't be working, maybe she could be with him. If she could be with Cliff, she did not want to spoil it by having a date with someone else. On the other hand, he probably would be working at Moore's Greenhouse again, and he definitely liked the Romans, so perhaps . . .

"Oh, I love school," Beatrice was saying with a laugh. For a moment, Betty was lost. Oh, yes, classes. That was what they'd been talking about. "I know it sounds odd," Beatrice went on, "but I've been crazy about school from the first day I went."

"I wish I could say that."

"You don't like it?"

"Or dislike it. It's school. Like vitamins. Good for you, so you take some every day and hope it's helping."

"Then why be so disapproving because Cliff doesn't like it?"

"Well, but Bea . . . people have to go to school."

"Cliff didn't."

"No. That's right, he didn't."

"For that matter, you don't have to take vitamins."

"No . . ." She didn't want to go on with this, because she did not want to remember, did not want to be reminded that Clifton hadn't finished high school. Why doesn't he go nights? she thought. Even if he does have to work in the day, he could have been going at night all this time. Eventually he'd get a high-school diploma, and then he could start going nights to college. . . .

"Cliff's a wonderful carpenter," Beatrice said. "And he knows more math than most engineers. Gil says so."

Carpenter, Betty said to herself with a shudder. Couldn't she say builder? Because that's what he is, practically. She corrected herself with stern realism. He's a carpenter and a handyman, and if you can't love him as he is, then give him up, because you aren't good enough for him. Her heart failed at the thought of ever having to give up Cliff and his love. He is so wonderful, she thought, and I just am not worthy.

Dazed and warm, she knew that, worthy or not, she had him. Had his heart, his thoughts, his first love. She felt strong as a goddess with power, and meek with the knowledge of how much more powerful than she was love.

"I wanted to tell you that I was sorry about Sunday," Beatrice said as they neared Perkins' Drugstore.

Oh, you needn't be sorry about Sunday, Betty said silently, not really talking to Bea. Last Sunday could not have been any way but the way it was. Beatrice had had to refuse her invitation, her mother had had to refuse her help in the garden, her father had had to suggest, in a kind, worried tone, that she take a nice walk, because he was upset about her and didn't know what else to suggest. All those things had had to be, just as Clifton was not really given a choice of which way he'd walk when he went out to shoot the crows he didn't shoot. It had all been ordained, and, Betty was inclined to think, ordained from the Creation, so that she and Clifton could meet at the little bridge and fall in love.

"I understand," she said warmly, and if the warmth in her voice was for another day, another person, Beatrice could not know that. "It's so busy at your house on Sunday. I should have known better."

"No, but it was awfully nice of you to ask me. We had relatives visiting, so I couldn't possibly have gotten away."

How would they know? Betty wondered with an inward giggle. So much family already there, how would relatives make themselves known? "That *must* have been a madhouse," she said so sympathetically that Beatrice burst into laughter.

"You were sort of overwhelmed that day, weren't you?"

Overrun, Betty thought. "Sort of. I guess . . . I seemed sort of standoffish or sulky or something. But, really, I just had never been with such a big family before."

"Well, now you know," Beatrice said, with a bright, vixenish look in her gray eyes. I dare you to like us, she challenged. I dare you to surrender to the barbarian hordes and be one of us, and we won't mend our manners, or make a special fuss for you, or remember that you've been brought up in gentle only-childness. Betty had the most unsettling feeling that Cliff, somehow, was included in this dare.

Take us all, including Clifton, as we are. That was the challenge.

All right, she thought. I accept.

"Are you having relatives this Sunday, too?" she asked. Beatrice shook her head. "Then, would you come to my house?"

"To jump and play?" Beatrice grinned.

"What?"

"Oh . . . it's a family joke. Gilda left a note for us once. She said, I've gone to my friend's house to jump and play. So now we practically always say it when we're going out."

"It's cute. Well, then, will you come to my house to jump and play?"

"I'd love to," said Beatrice.

After that they spent part of nearly every Sunday together. If Cliff was not working, he would drive Betty to the Romans' or Beatrice to the Wilders', but often they used buses or Mrs. Wilder's car because Cliff had so little time apart from work. What he had, he gave to Betty, but there was not enough of it.

Since he had left school, Cliff had been accustomed to working long and steadily. Jobs on Sundays and holidays were routine, extra work at night seemed to him only normal. And the Bankses, mother and son, were provident. They put money in the bank, and they not only went without luxuries, it seemed to Betty they went without necessities. It was not for her to say, and she never did, but a girl brought up by parents who spent everything that came in as it came in could not help wondering at people who would save before they bought themselves clothes, or a car, or nice things for their house.

"They never spend anything," she said to her father one evening, after Cliff had telephoned to say he was held up on a job. She was annoyed and disappointed, and trying not to show it.

"Good for them."

"I'm serious."

"So am I. I wish I never spent anything."

"Daddy, you don't mean that."

"I mean it, in a way. Not enough to do anything about it, of course. But, then, it's too late for me. I'm committed to shiftlessness."

"I don't think it's shiftless to want to live gracefully."

"Shiftless is what they call it, honey, when you get more graceful than your bank account." He smiled at her worried look. "Don't take me literally. I'm managing my minuet with the First National, and I guess I won't fall on my face. I just get mild attacks of conscience when I see people like Cliff and his mother laying away for the rainy day."

"Oh, pooh. Suppose you do all that laying away and the rainy day never comes."

"If there is one thing you can depend on, it's that the rainy day will roll around."

"I'd rather get my feet wet when it rains than go around in rubbers all the time the sun is shining."

"I'd say," her father commented with great amusement, "that we've managed to overlook the existence of rubbers pretty handily. What's the matter, anyway? You mad at Cliff? Does he seem stingy to you?"

"Oh, no," Betty said quickly, bristling at any criticism of Clifton. "That isn't what I meant. I just meant I'm glad we're not that way. But it's all right if they—if he —is. Are." She looked confused. "He isn't at all stingy, he's just careful. People are different, you know."

"I know," he said soberly. "They are, and a good thing, too, as we're reminded from time to time. Cliff's a fine boy. And, of course, he has to think about his mother. He'll probably have to take care of her one day. I daresay with all his labor and hers they don't make more than a little less than enough." He brooded a moment. "He's the most self-confident nineteen-year-old I've met in many a day. Nice to meet someone without that ubiquitous complex."

"What complex?"

"Inferiority," he said. "Every time science wipes out a new disease, the inferiority complex hurries to fill the gap. If this keeps up, we'll all be too healthy to die and too morbid and timid to live. What a prospect!"

Betty agreed it would be terrible, if true, and Mr. Wilder accused her of not having an inferiority complex herself. "And I don't think your mother has either. Which leaves me holding the bag."

Betty laughed. "I don't believe a word of it."

"Oh. I'll agree that in the business world I'm known far and wide as a man with a mind of his own. A pretty warlike fellow, in fact. But, aside from business . . . oh, me. Of course, when the super race arrives, the inferiorty complex will be as curious and obsolete as the sweating sickness. But we won't be around for that, or our great-grandchildren, either."

"The super race will be a long time coming?"

Mr. Wilder looked thoughtful. "I doubt," he said finally, "if they'll make it at all. Not if they have to evolve from this one."

Betty liked talking to her father when he was in this slightly magisterial, pseudo-cynical mood. She would have hated real cynicism, but, she told herself, since he's no more cynical than he's insecure, it's fun to hear him ramble this way. Her enjoyment dissipated, for a while, the disappointment of not seeing Cliff.

"What's the sweating sickness?" she said.

"A disease prevalent in the fifteenth and sixteenth centuries. It wiped out half the population of England."

"I think we're already a super race," Betty said. "The things that we survive. Sweating sickness, witch hunts, wars. How would we last, if we weren't super? And the way we hurt each other. I mean, each other's feelings. We have to be strong to survive that."

"We are strong. And we're stubborn. And we're able to be blind when we can't stand what we see, and deaf when we can't stand what we hear. But that's not being superior, it's hanging on because we have to." He sighed and then put the whole conception from him, with an almost physical gesture. "Tell me, what other young men are you seeing besides Cliff? Haven't heard of anyone except him since I've been home this time."

"Other? None."

"That's a change, isn't it?" he asked, after a pause.

Betty didn't answer. She did not propose to tell her parents that she loved Clifton Banks, that it was a serious, adult love, a love that couldn't possibly admit other relationships, the way her superficial, young girl's love for George had. She would have thought they'd guess, but never would she say it to them.

"Isn't it?" her father persisted.

"Isn't what what?"

"Betty, you heard what I said. Isn't it a change for you to concentrate on just one boy? You know I don't like this going-steady business. You're too young for that sort of thing."

"I'll be eighteen soon," she said nervously, repelled by the expression *going steady*. She was not going steady with Cliff. She loved him. More than life, for all her life. Going steady was a child's game. You could go steady with someone for a year or a day or for fifteen minutes. It didn't mean anything except a kind of social insurance, subject to change without notice, cancelable at the drop (or return) of a pin. You don't know what you're talking about, she said to her father silently, wishing she hadn't stayed downstairs to talk to him.

She got to her feet. "I'd better go up and study. I'll be at it till dawn as it is."

"I realize you're putting me off," he said. "But I'd like to make myself clear. I do not approve of your limiting yourself to one boy."

Cliff isn't a boy, she protested, but knew better than to say it aloud. "I thought you liked Cliff."

"I do like him. I like him very much. I just don't want anyone monopolizing your youth."

It's my youth, isn't it? Who are you to decide what I'm going to do with my youth? I'll bet you didn't let your father tell you what to do with yours.

She shifted in the doorway, not wanting to antagonize him, not wanting to answer him. If she eased away, neither agreeing nor disagreeing, chances were he'd forget. He was on the road a lot, and didn't really keep track of her comings and goings. It all comes, she told herself sternly, of *talking* too much. I love Cliff so much that I can't stop talking about him. But maybe now I'll stop. You really had to be on your guard every minute, but once you knew it, all right—stay on guard. "I guess I see what you mean," she offered carefully. That was really saying nothing at all, but perhaps he wouldn't notice.

"I hope you do," he said tonelessly, and allowed her to leave by picking up his newspaper.

But what Betty didn't understand was that no more than she wanted it did her father want to antagonize her. He said as much to his wife when she came in from watering the lawn.

"*Have* you antagonized her?" Mrs. Wilder asked.

"I guess so. At least, I don't know. How can I tell? One minute she was sitting here and we were having a nice talk, and the next thing she was pleading homework and fluttering in the door like a chicken wing."

"Well, you must have said something."

"I said I didn't want her going steady with Cliff Banks."

"Oh."

"What's the significance of that oh?"

Mrs. Wilder closed her eyes for a moment, then opened and fixed them on her husband with an expression of sad patience. "I guess it signifies that the battle's been lost before it ever was engaged." She winced a little at the word engaged. "What I mean is, it's too late to tell her not to go steady with Cliff. She is. I fancy she finds it a good deal more important than what going steady would imply."

"What do you mean?" he almost screamed. "She's going to marry him?"

"Calm down. I mean, there's no use saying anything at this point. They're young and they're very much in love. Can't you see that? Weren't you ever young and very much in love?"

"No." He stared at her. "Yes. With you."

"Even before that," she said easily. "When you feel that way, you don't want to make dates with other people. And your father's rantings can only—" she looked at him steadily "—only make it worse. I hope I make myself clear."

"You make yourself clear," he said wearily. "Will she get over it?"

"I don't know. She could go farther and do worse."

"She's too young."

"That's what *I'm* saying. Don't stampede young hearts."

"You needn't be so melodramatic."

"You needn't be so precipitous. Girls have loved this much before, and lived to love again, and love again."

"I hope you're right." He stared around the room in helpless anger. "He hasn't even finished high school."

"Is that a remark that's worthy of you?"

"Yes. I think it is. Betty will be a well-educated girl. What are they going to talk about if they marry?"

"Who says they're getting married?"

"*You* did." He stopped in confusion. "Oh, I don't know what I'm talking about."

"You were saying, most unfairly, that they wouldn't have anything to talk about because he hasn't finished high school. He's a lot brighter and more interesting than plenty of college graduates I've met."

"Where's his ambition?"

"Answer that yourself. Have you ever seen anyone work harder? That boy will be something someday. And even if he weren't it's not your affair."

"Not my affair if he wants to marry my daughter?"

"Oh, you're hopeless. Has he requested her hand from you yet? No. Well, I daresay he's the old-fashioned type who would. You're getting me nervous with your talk of marriage. They're two young people in love and there's every chance they'll get over it, and if they don't we'll face that then."

"Let's look at Wyatt Earp."

"He isn't on tonight."

"Then let's go out and paint the town."

"Paint *Norwood?*"

"Then let's play Scrabble. I'm sick of thinking."

"All right. You get out the board."

"She isn't the same at all," he said, not moving. "She doesn't have phone calls and crowds of girls, even, the way she used to. And don't say I used to fuss about the phone. I know I used to fuss about the phone. I wish I were in a position to fuss again."

"She sees Beatrice," his wife said pityingly. "You like her."

"Beatrice is a lovely girl. But she's just one girl. I want things to be the way they used to be. *Lots* of people, and not all this concentration, don't you see?"

"Yes," she said. "I do see. Well . . . since you won't get the Scrabble board, I will. Where did we put it last time we played? Do you remember?"

"You aren't answering?"

"There's nothing to say."

In a motion of defeat, Mr. Wilder gestured toward the hall closet. "We left it in there," he said. "I'll get it."

10

"I LOVE YOU, I LOVE YOU, I love you," she whispered, nestling against him.

"And I do you." He held her close. "Getting cold?"

"No. Well, maybe a little."

"We'll go soon."

But they remained, close to each other in the chilly cab of the truck, looking at the snowy fields bright in the moon. Their breaths mingled. A dog in the distance barked. His bark was sharp in the cold air, and Clifton lifted his head to listen.

"What are you thinking?" he asked, after a while.

"That I'll huff and I'll puff and I'll blow your heart in."

"It went down at the first breath."

"Then I'll build it up again."

"You've done that, too."

They'd been to the movies, and afterward had a hot chocolate, and now on their way home they stopped to look at the snowy fields and tell each other, as they had told it so many times before, their love. Now and then he kissed her gently, and only once with a fierce assurance that he checked almost before she could respond.

He's very different from the other boys, she thought. He's not, as I once told Daddy, a boy at all. But I'm sure he's very different from other young men, too. He doesn't paw or gobble. Not that the boys she had known were like that. At least, as soon as she'd realize they were, she'd bid them a quick unyielding good-by. She didn't like to be pawed or gobbled at.

"What can you expect?" Carol used to say. "A certain amount of that you have to put up with."

"I don't."

"Oh, stop."

She could tell Carol didn't quite believe her, and she saw no advantage in insisting. But, whatever Carol did or didn't do, Betty Wilder had held hands and, once in awhile, not often, been kissed, not hard.

She wanted from Cliff more than his tender kisses, his gentle restrained caresses. She wanted what lay behind the rare, suddenly urgent and demanding embraces that he so quickly checked. Yet she loved him more for knowing he would not yield to that urgency, that demand. She loved him because he was both aggressor and protector, and she knew that in him the protector was always uppermost, so she was safe to circle the edges of a glorious but real danger. He would not draw her into its perilous center.

Yet tonight, in the creaking, windy, moon-wan cold, she was content to be held in his arms, moveless, dreamy, a little numb from the chill air that even the motor, kept running, could not dispel.

"Have you ever thought," she murmured, "that you could take a whole lifetime getting to know just one person?"

"Is that what we're going to do?"

"I hope so," she said, snuggling. "It's what I want. But if you don't think about a person and watch and wonder about him and *care*, how would you ever know that he likes the sound of dogs barking far away?"

He tipped her chin up and looked into her eyes. "How did you know that I like that?"

"From caring about you. You get a sort of thinking, faraway look. You did a little while ago."

"What a strange thing, for you to know that. There's something . . . sort of homey and wild at the same time in the sound of a dog barking far away. When I was a kid, I used to stop to listen, and think, That fellow's standing in somebody's yard, guarding it, making the world know he's on the job, and here am I, all this distance away, listening to him and he doesn't know it. Used to make me feel funny. Good, but sort of peculiar. As if I didn't know anything. And when I was a kid—" he grinned—"most of the time I was pretty sure I knew everything."

"I guess everybody has those things in their lives. I mean, that mean an enormous amount to them but don't make sense to anyone else. The way I feel about the smell of gingersnaps."

"How do you?" His voice was full of tender curiosity, as it was about anything that concerned her.

"Well, it's hard to explain. But I do know that the smell of gingersnaps has an effect on me like catnip on a kitten. I don't mean I chase around madly, but it transports me. The first whiff does. If I smell them too long, the feeling goes away. But the first whiff of a gingersnap is magic to me. I suppose it's something that happened in my childhood. That makes me feel this way, I mean."

"You could probably trace it back."

"But I don't want to. I want to be enraptured by the smell of gingersnaps and never know the reason why. If I knew, maybe I wouldn't feel that way any more."

"Why do you love me?"

"I don't know," she said dreamily. "So many reasons. How can you tell why you're in love?"

"Then if you knew the reasons, maybe you wouldn't love me any more?"

She twisted out of his arms and faced him indignantly. "Clifton Banks, you tricked me. That was a low, low thing to do."

He smiled at her happily, dwellingly. She could feel his delight in her, sense without words the keen pleasure he took in looking at her, listening to her. It was the headiest knowledge she had ever had, this of power to enchant, to bewitch, another human being. And she knew, through some natural instinct, when to prolong such a moment, when to let it melt gently away, leaving traces of something savored, but not to satiety. This was a time to spin out. He was still willingly tangled in the threads of love and allure she wove about him.

"Apologize," she said sternly.

"Forgive me," he said, then leaned over and whispered in her ear, "Let *me* be your gingersnap."

They fell into each other's arms laughing, and then grew quieter, and then utterly quiet. She ran her finger in a circle around the palm of his hand and their breathing grew deep and unsteady. They did not look at each other.

Clifton sighed. "It's cold, my love. And I must get you home."

"All right," she said docilely.

She had the power to bewitch, but Clifton made the decisions.

It was true that she knew, from loving him, things she would never have troubled to learn about any other person. She probed and inquired and watched and listened. She weighed and considered him, went over, in her mind, his temper and caprices. He had very few caprices, and a rather steady temper that in someone not Cliff she might have called phlegmatic. He was a listener. With his pleasant half-smile, his half-closed eyes (that meant he was relaxing), he would listen while she told him of school, of Chicago, of Carol (never of George, or Weldon, or Matthew), of her intentions and regrets and resolutions.

"Why don't you tell *me* things?" she complained one day. "You sit there like Buddha, listening to me tell my —what do they call it?—my hopes, my dreams, my fears. And what do you say?"

"Right now I say I have to get to work."

"You *can't* have to get to work. It's four o'clock on Saturday afternoon. Nobody goes to work at four o'clock on Saturday afternoon."

"Betty, darling. I've been with you since noon."

"What am I supposed to do? Get down on my knees and say thank you, thank you, master, for these hours, I'll live on their memory through the long winter months—"

"Gil called this morning and said Mr. Perone could use us on an extra job. Gil's going to pick me up. I told you when I came in."

"No, you didn't."

"You didn't listen."

"Blast Gil, and Mr. Perone, too," she said, close to tears. "I thought we were going to have the whole *day*."

"Well, we can't." He kissed her gently on the temple. "I love you, Betty."

She knew, from loving him and being angry at him, from lashing out and holding her tongue and finding it came to the same thing, that Cliff was going to work harder, longer hours than anyone else she had ever known, that he was not going to alter this, nor propitiate her because he didn't.

"I have to," he'd say unemphatically. "It's a job."

"Get a normal job. Get a job like other people, from nine to five, five days a week," she flared.

He didn't lose his temper, he did not explain that a man's work was his own decision, he did not tell her she was interfering where she had no right to interfere. He simply went to work.

That day when he left, Betty went up to her room and sank in a chair, determined to think this matter out. Staring at a speck on the floor (a bit of cotton? A shred of Kleenex?), she clamped her mind on the subject of Cliff's work as if it were a piece of metal she could put in a vise and hammer into some more pleasing shape.

She'd known from the beginning, hadn't she, that he did not have a job like other people, that he had a multiplicity of jobs that kept him busy for longer than anyone had a right to be (certainly than anyone in love had a right to be), and since she had known it, why couldn't she accept it gracefully? I can't, she muttered angrily, because nobody could. It's worse than being in love with a doctor . . . at least you can figure a doctor is doing somebody else some good while he's neglecting you. What good is Cliff doing? He's doing a lot of good, she rebuked herself, as irritably as if someone else had impugned him. He builds fine, strong, useful things . . . barns and buildings and greenhouses. What do you mean, he builds? He hammers nails where somebody else tells him to hammer them. Oh, but you're *small*, she told herself scornfully. You've always thought your mind so roomy, your outlook so inclusive. You're a small-minded person. He's nineteen years old. Of course somebody else has to tell him where the nails go. In time he'll know better than they do. Probably he does already, but who lets a nineteen-year-old tell them anything? For that matter, how do you know they *don't* let him tell them? You don't know what he does on a job. What *is* that thing on the floor?

She shook her head, got back to Cliff. He works and he works and he works. He puts money in the bank, presumably. He's good to his mother. He's a credit to youth, and he makes me miserable, she concluded with a dry sob. He leaves me without even seeming to mind, he forgets to call, he . . .

Oh, stop, stop, stop . . .

I must make an effort to understand, she told herself, getting up to see what the thing on the floor was. A bit of Kleenex, just as she'd thought. She tossed it into the basket. I must make myself see this from his point of view, since clearly he is not going to see it from mine. She remembered saying once, oh, long long ago, that for love you said, However he wants me, that way will I be. Well, then, *be* how he wants you to be. Patient, sympathetic, forgiving, uncomplaining when he has to work, when he has to leave you, even though you'd planned on having him with you. But the very listing of these qualities made her furious all over again. Who was Cliff, who was any boy, to expect that from a girl? What, for pity's sake, did they give in return? Again she relented. He expected nothing of the sort. He wanted her as she was, and gave her everything. What sort of person *was* she, to talk of returns? You don't look for returns in love, you only want to love. Ideally, you'd be willing not even to receive love in turn. The giving would be enough. But this was an idea Betty could only glance at, not conceivably assimilate.

Like a moth at a window, she beat her wings against the indissoluble, and eventually fell down spent.

She was lying on her bed, examining the ceiling, when she heard her father and mother drive in. She went down to help them carry in groceries.

"You've certainly gotten to be peculiarly helpful around the house," Mr. Wilder complained.

"My pleasure, Daddy."

"You weren't this way in Chicago."

"Lots of things have changed since Chicago."

"They certainly have," he sighed.

Mr. Wilder, when he was home, asked nicely after Cliff, greeted him cordially, said "Fine boy, that," when he thought Betty was apt to hear. He never made any direct reference to the evening of his abortive attempt to terminate, or anyway lessen, the closeness between Cliff and his daughter. Betty didn't know whether her mother had talked to him, he'd given up or given in, he didn't care any more, or was biding his time. She did not, in truth, worry much about it. Helpless before Cliff's determination to know his own mind, she felt quite capable of parrying or withstanding any such attitude on her father's part. Cliff might leave her dateless half the Saturday nights of her life, but her father couldn't make her date someone else. Cliff might call when she least expected it and forget to call when she was waiting for the bell like a tensed boxer, but her father could not make her welcome any other voice on the phone.

She thought there was something sad in the way young people reached a point where their parents (once omnipotent, unrefusable, without flaw) could no longer influence them. Sad, but there was nothing you could or would do about it. Once the crown has slipped, you no longer obey the king, though of course you can love his person all your life.

Betty sometimes felt she loved her father and mother

more since she was, in a sense, leaving them. And she was glad, grateful, to have had so many years of holding her parents in such high esteem. Not that she esteemed them less now . . . she simply did not need them in the old way. I'm glad that I did need them, she thought, and that they never—hardly ever—left my need unanswered. Carol, who didn't care for hers, and George, who ignored his, may have seemed freer, but I was surer.

"Heard anything from George or Carol?" said her father, putting a pot of coffee on to percolate.

"Isn't that funny, I was just thinking of them."

"Should think you would. They're your best friends, aren't they?"

Oh, Daddy, poor Daddy, she mourned. He just will not give in. George and Carol are the past to him, everything that he complained about and relished in the past, and he keeps hoping to meet them (or their very counterparts) every time he turns a corner.

"They used to be, Daddy. Time marches on, you know."

"Time is a hangman," said Mr. Wilder. "Where's the cream? Didn't we buy any cream? Oh, thanks. . . . A hangman. Loop, loop, loop, and there are the friends of yesteryear, dangling on the gibbet. Time marches on, for God's sake. What about friendship? I bet you don't even write to them any more."

"They aren't dangling on a gibbet. They're in Chicago and I'm here. And we don't write as much as we used to, but we still write. How many friends of yours are left in Chicago that you don't see any more?"

"At least I've made some new ones."

"So have I," she said coolly. "As a matter of fact, I like everybody I know, which is probably more than you can say."

"Liking *everybody* is just a more personal way of being detached."

"Oh, Daddy, you're impossible to please." She looked to her mother for help.

"How is Jack Roman?" said Mrs. Wilder. "Has he found a valuable yet?"

Betty laughed with an effort. (What was she going

to *do* for the rest of the afternoon, the evening?) "He says he's about given up on that. Because his mother won't let him take a reward if he does find anything. Now he's written away for a book on hidden treasures. It seems there are treasures buried all over the place, all you have to do is get where they are and start digging."

"I know that book." Mr. Wilder grinned. "Thought of having a go at it myself, but what can you do with a wife who won't go to the seashore and pirates who wouldn't go anywhere else?"

"Get a shovel and we'll leave tomorrow," said Mrs. Wilder. "If that's what will make you happy."

"What do you mean, if that's what will make me happy? Am I so hard to please? I think I'm an extraordinarily reasonable man. A pipe, a pup, and a Morris chair, and you've got a happy man. Why don't we get a dog?"

"Or a Morris chair," said his wife.

"What's a Morris chair?" said Betty.

"Before your time, dear," her father explained. "We used to use them for spooning. The expression is somewhat out of date." He broke off sharply, and Betty knew he was wondering about her and Cliff and what he chose to call spooning.

"The expression," said Mrs. Wilder, "was out of date before your time, too. You make me feel about eighty."

"That's nothing to what I feel," he said.

"For a reasonable man," she pointed out, "you lapse into unmanageability rather quickly."

Betty was putting away groceries, her attention only half caught by their words. She had, in these months, come to be what her mother had implored her, over the years, to be—a help around the house. She cleaned, changed linen, did dishes, helped with the cooking, all without being urged, without underlining the fact that she was doing it. They would never know, and it did not concern them, that she did it in an effort to be the person she thought Cliff would want her to be.

She pretended he could see her, as she went about these mundane tasks so willingly and prettily. She pretended, as a matter of fact, that he could always see her.

She tried to keep her motions at all times graceful, her voice gentle, her manner polished. She was unremittingly lovable, helpful, sweet. Except, of course, when she forgot, or when she was angry with Cliff, but these moods were so transient that Mr. and Mrs. Wilder scarcely saw them. They were presented with a daughter whom anyone would call a girl to pattern by, and they were less thankful than baffled.

"What's she doing this for?" Mr. Wilder would ask his wife covertly when Betty rose from the table and began to clear the dishes, refusing help. "What is this all about?"

"Hush. I don't know."

"One thing *I* know . . . To be killed with kindness is no mere phrase."

"Take advantage of it. Enjoy it while you can."

"You don't seem to be enjoying it."

"Well, I'm not. I'm too confused. But don't say anything."

And they'd break off, flustered, when Betty came back from the kitchen, urging them to go away and just sit, take it easy. They'd go into the living room, anything but easy, and sit, while Betty, occupied with showing off for an invisible Cliff, forgot about them as she gracefully did the dishes.

It's not, she'd tell herself, singing and soaping and rinsing and stacking, that I like this sort of thing, or intend to keep it up forever. It's just that . . . it's just that I love you, my darling, and I might as well be doing this, since I can't be with you. It pleases Mother and Daddy, and I can be alone and think about you, and miss you, and long for you. . . . Over and over in her mind she said, Clifton, I love you, I am so much in love with you.

There had not been, since that day at the bridge, a single waking moment (and very few, she thought, when I'm asleep) that she was not conscious of Cliff. He was in her mind always. When she was with people, when she was alone, when she worked or rested or played or dreamed, always there was Cliff, and his voice, and his words, and the look in his blue eyes when they rested on her face.

136

She scarcely knew, so lost to time and the world was she, that the winter was bitter, and then that the winter was past. She'd sledded on two or three starry nights with him, and walked a long way in a white wild storm, and given him, at Christmas, a beautiful, terribly expensive keyring that now he was never without. She'd wakened mornings to see snow piled against the windows in triangles, and rain flinging against the panes, sliding down in slow, hanging patterns, and sun, pale as grapefruit for weeks, falling in a square on her blanket and the floor.

No matter what the morning—snowy, rainy, sunny —Cliff came by in his truck to drive her to school, and every morning he left her two blocks away, though they'd long stopped telling each other that that way he didn't have to turn around.

It was the one time that she could depend on seeing him, those mornings he drove her to school. On weekends, or when she was on vacation, he was apt to have jobs that took him away much earlier (the produce for the stand he bought each morning, earlier still), and once he went with Gil and Mr. Perone on a job that kept him away a week. He wrote her one note. It had two misspellings in it. She threw it into the fire and cried half the night for wanting it, for hating herself.

And so she worked at school, and around the house was helpful and lovable and baffling (though she did not know that) and saw the Romans, and got accepted in one of the colleges of her choice.

But she was not fooled. She knew that all she really did was wait for the time when she could be with Cliff, remember and relive the time when it was over, and wait for the next time.

Now on a mid-spring afternoon, while her father and mother sat at the table and drank coffee and half-teased each other, she put away the groceries and wondered what to do with the rest of the day since Clifton was gone, once again, on a job. The afternoon, the evening stretched before her like a punishment. She felt pinched and tired, too flat even to carry on the little game of showing off for the invisible Cliff. Because, she told herself drearily, he really *is* invisible. Invisible and gone, and no more thinking of me than—than anyone else is, she finished in a spurt of self-pity. Why show off for someone who's looking the other way? She put the things away because she'd started to, because it wasn't her parents' fault that Cliff preferred his job to her, because she couldn't think of anything else to do.

If this is love, she said to herself (there were hours and hours and *hours* still to be got through somehow), if this is love, I'll take cyanide.

"Darling," said Mrs. Wilder to her husband, "let's go to New York some night and mambo."

"Mambo!" he yelled. "I just finished saying I'm the Morris-chair type. You must understand that I, my dear, am loyal to Vernon Castle."

Betty listened to them with a pitying fondness. They were so far far away from all that was meaningful and real in life. From love and desire, even from the pain of missing someone as she now missed Cliff, they were released.

She decided that, with all its anguish, she'd take love. Because . . . a feeling of triumph lifted her on a giddy wave . . . because I am young, I love and am loved, and tomorrow Clifton will come back to me.

In a wild wide arc her pendulum swung, and for dear life she hung on.

11

MR. GORHAM, THE WORLD History teacher, who was just as aware as his students that this was the last class on a Friday afternoon, suppressed a yawn he'd caught from Joe Preston, who hadn't troubled to suppress his, and said thickly, "Rosecrans would be an example—"

Example? Betty thought. Example of what? Who's Rosecrans? She glanced down at her notebook, in which she appeared to have jotted a few things, then looked more closely, hoping to find out what they were talking about. Nothing about Rosecrans there. Oh well, he had something to do with the Civil War, since the whole period had to do with the Civil War. She could look him up later. She looked at her watch. Twenty minutes to go.

The windows were open and the airs of spring

moved in disturbingly. She could hear the band practicing out on the football field, cars arriving and departing in the parking lot. A couple of teachers went by in the hall. Betty watched them idly through a window in the door. One she didn't recognize, the other was her English teacher, whom she couldn't abide.

She had mentioned this to her father, who had (what else?) immediately asked if she couldn't try to see the teacher's side of things.

"No. I can't. And I think you carry that business too far. You can't always be seeing someone else's side and never your own. Where this particular teacher and I are concerned, it's a personality clash, period. Did you get along with all your teachers?"

"Splendidly," he said, but had the conscience to avoid her eyes.

"Flimflam," she'd replied, using one of his own favorite words.

And flimflam it was. Sometimes she thought her father one of the most unrealistic men in the world. Especially where education was concerned. School was a temple, teachers sacrosanct, learning above rubies. She supposed unhappily that it was one of the reasons he objected to Cliff. It couldn't be just the going-steady objection. There must be more to it than that, and what could the more be but Clifton's two solitary years of high school, and Clifton's obvious indifference to any more?

Since it pained her too much to think about this, she circled back to carp at her father's attitude about the English teacher. This always seeing everyone else's side of everything. "Keep an open mind," says Daddy, "keep that mind *open*." Well, I'm willing enough in the ordinary way to keep my mind open, but when I have to listen to Mrs. X for forty minutes every day, it just closes up again in self-defense. The trouble with Daddy is he's never faced the fact that while there are some good teachers, and some mediocre teachers, there are some teachers who are just plain bad. And Mrs. X is their prophet.

This teacher, Mr. Gorham of World History, was

good. But he was also yawning. And it was Friday, the last class of the day. And it was spring. She looked at her watch again. Seven minutes.

Joe Preston put his arms down at his sides and stretched them mightily. He yawned stupefyingly, not bothering to cover his mouth. Betty saw Mr. Gorham's look of intense annoyance, but Joe saw nothing. He'd closed his eyes. Giving his profile a moment's speculative, unmoved appraisal, she thought, If he were better-looking he'd be handsome.

". . . and so," said Mr. Gorham, closing his book, "if each of you over the week end will write a thousand words on a forgotten man of history . . ."

Forgotten man, Betty thought indignantly. If they've forgotten how can we find out about them? The things these teachers dream up—

"This class is dismissed," said Mr. Gorham. Though it lacked three minutes of the bell, he'd gone as far as he could.

Joe Preston put a detaining hand on Betty's desk. "You remind me of Brier Rose," he said. "Wasn't it Brier Rose who sat in the middle of all those thorns, waiting to be rescued?"

"Maybe Brier Rose did," she laughed.

She'd tried to put dismissal in her tone, but he didn't move. She had heard that Joe and Ginny were no longer a couple, but hoped he wouldn't elect to honor her next. For one thing, she found it difficult to explain why she was so unavailable at school—and she had had already to explain to a couple of boys this year. She had not explained directly, or even correctly (Cliff was so much a part of another world, so little related to Norwood High, that naming him would mean nothing, so she had simply been evasive), and she had to admit that they had not been very persistent.

Joe, on the other hand, might be. She knew his type, had known, even when he was still going with Ginny, the import of the glances he sent her way. He was self-satisfied, pleasant, and probably used to having his own way. He was, in fact, quite a bit like George, which put her at a disadvantage, because she had a feeling of already knowing him and so could not be downright curt. It would be like being curt to George, which would be just plain silly, Cliff or no Cliff.

So she smiled at him, as if he were George, and began to explain (as she certainly would have if he *had* been George) that her life was quite complicated, but she stood in no need of rescue. She took her books, waved, and walked away.

Joe fell into step beside her. "Great to see the spring come, isn't it?"

"Oh, it is," she sighed happily. "I love it."

These high-skied sunny mornings, tangled with birdsongs, when the fresh breezes lifted the curtains at her windows and lifted her heart and lifted her father's voice in song, were glorious, A slate-gray catbird, elegant and trim as a marquise, sang on a bough of the willow tree in their back yard, and in his shower her father boomed and gurgled. . . .

"Oh, Shenandoah, I luhuve your dahaughter . . . way hey, you rrrrolling ruhiver . . ."

And Clifton, Clifton, Clifton . . . He drove up in his old truck newly washed, his face bright and sweet, his sleeves rolled up on his beautiful arms, and he said, "Good morning, Betty," and she said, "Good morning, Cliff, good morning," and the day began with sun and singing and Clifton.

Of course she loved the spring and its coming.

"I adore it," she said. Her face was filled with love, and Joe Preston made a natural mistake.

"Look, Betty," he said. "I've been wanting to ask you . . ."

"Ask me what?" she said. It was probably the wrong thing to say, but, on the other hand, suppose he didn't have in mind what she thought he had in mind. Suppose he wanted to ask her if she remembered a forgotten man in history. It would be pretty face-losing to say no before he said please.

He said it. "I wanted to ask if you'd go out with me. How about tonight, for instance?"

"Oh, Joe . . . I *can't*."

But she was so full of fondness, of spring, so ripe

142

with affection for the world, that he went right on confusing her intention.

"Tomorrow night, then. We could have a ball."

She almost asked, out of plain curiosity, Have a ball doing what? Having a ball in Norwood seemed to Betty (and her mother) like having a ball on an iceberg.

"What in the world do people do here?" Mrs. Wilder complained. "I mean, if you don't like bowling or movies, where are you and what do you do?"

Betty could have answered, You do nothing, unless you're in love. Then, of course, anything . . . driving bricks across county, going out to shoot crows, riding double on broad old Calvin along lazy roads, going to the movies, just sitting in the truck and talking . . . anything is good, if you're in love.

But she said to her mother, "I suppose people go to New York."

"How about it?" Joe was saying impatiently.

"How about what? I'm sorry."

"Boy, Brier Rose isn't the word for you. And as for *thorns* . . ."

He must have been reading a book or something, Betty thought unkindly. Maybe he's heard my father's in publishing and he's getting at me through shop talk.

She became aware of his furious silence. "Sorry," she repeated. "No, Joe, I really can't. You see—" She saw Beatrice coming toward her and gave an overenthusiastic wave. "There's Beatrice."

"I'm not blind."

"I mean, we're supposed to meet. She has something she wants to tell me." She hurried forward. "I've been *looking* for you." With a wave and a bright smile, she indicated to Joe that now she was fine. As if he'd been seeing me to the train, she giggled to herself, and said softly to Beatrice, "Start walking and act in a hurry."

"What's it all about?" Beatrice asked breathlessly when they were outdoors. "I take it we're escaping from Joe Preston?"

"We are."

"Well, I'm here to tell you, you aren't going to escape if you keep on looking at him the way you were looking at him."

"What do you mean?"

"Your face was glowing. It was alight with kindness and sweet indulgence."

"Oh, it was not."

"Yes."

"I just feel good, that's all. I feel wonderful. I can't look as if I didn't feel wonderful if I do feel wonderful, can I?"

"I'm only pointing out that Joe will be coming around until you explain *very* clearly that the look is not for him."

"I did explain. I told him I couldn't go out with him."

"You looked as if you were saying, Darling, I can't go out with you, dearest."

Betty laughed. "Did I? Well, next time I'll frown."

"After the treatment you gave him today, you'd better stamp on his foot."

"I never can understand that kind of boy, the sort who's so sure he's the answer to any girl's problem. You practically never find a girl who feels she's the answer for *all* boys."

"I think it's their mothers."

"Whose mothers?"

"The boys'. Mothers make their sons feel princely and irresistible. I suppose they think they are. Look at how my mother behaves with Gil and Jack and Harry and Parm. And Woojums, too, only he's too young to be fooled. But the others . . . Don't you think Mama acts as if lordlings were on the scene when the boys are around? And does she treat *us* that way? Gilda and Cora and me, I mean. She loves us, but I'd certainly never get the impression from Mama that the world was my oyster, and the only one of the boys who *doesn't* think it is is Jack. His sense of humor is too good."

It was true. The Roman boys swaggered. Charming, disarming swaggerers, but maddening. Gil had merely to lift a brow and the world would come running, he thought. Generally, Betty had to agree that it did. His world. Gil didn't seem to be aware of how small a one it was, but Betty sometimes wondered how he'd fare if he left Norwood and his family, the townspeople with whom he'd grown up, and the employers who knew him so well.

Beatrice was probably right about mothers. They somehow made their sons believe that a mother's valuation was the world's. Mrs. Banks was not like that with Cliff, but Mrs. Banks did not seem to Betty at all a usual mother. She was more like a hard-working, laconic, unsentimental partner. She'd speak of Cliff with pride and energy, but never with softness, never with a woman's nostalgia for the child this man had been.

"I don't suppose," she said now to Beatrice, "that Mrs. Banks will ever like me."

"No," said Beatrice bluntly. "I guess not. Falling in love was not one of the plans she had for Cliff, and that I know."

"But people can't make that sort of plan for their children."

"They can try. I've known the Bankses forever, and Mrs. Banks has never had anything in mind for him but work and economy."

"What about his happiness?"

"Well, to be honest, I think she figures that is his happiness. Working. It was, you know, until he met you. I'm not surprised she resents you. I seem to be generalizing about mothers, but Mama hates on the spot any girl Gil seems interested in, and he's never been really in love, the way Cliff is with you."

Betty's fancy caught and caressed the words, the delicious knowledge that Cliff's love was so open. She didn't mind what Mrs. Banks thought. It would be nice to have her affection, but it wasn't necessary.

Her mother had said one day, "You know, Mrs. Banks isn't as agreeable as she used to be. Do you suppose it's because of Cliff's attention to you?"

Betty had shrugged. "I suppose." Against the shield of her love, the hostility of Mrs. Banks was useless, an arrow of straw.

"How do you feel about her? Do you dislike her?"

"I never think about her enough to find out."

"I tell myself," said Mrs. Wilder slowly, "that young people have to be hard sometimes. I tell myself it's their defense against the advantages of age."

Betty hadn't replied.

"I'll walk you over to Perkins'," she said now to Beatrice.

"Oh. Well, that's what I wanted to tell you. I've quit."

"Quit? Why?"

Beatrice gave her a half-amused, half-confounded glance, and said, "It's confusing. I'm trying to think how to tell Mama."

"Tell Mama what? Maybe I could help, if I knew what you were talking about."

"Well . . . Mr. Perkins asked me to marry him."

"Marry him!" Betty burst out. "Mr. *Perkins?* But he's *old.*"

"He isn't thirty yet," said Beatrice, faintly protective of her unwanted suitor.

"He looks a lot more than that."

"That's because he's so colorless." Beatrice turned judicious. "Age is more a matter of thin blood than of wrinkles, I think. Mr. Perkins doesn't have wrinkles, but he's sort of pale in the bloodstream, or something."

"You certainly took your time about telling me."

"I'm not just dying to talk about it, that's why."

"Marry Mr. Perkins," Betty said, bemused. "My goodness."

"Well, it's sort of a shame to have your first proposal be from Mr. Perkins, to say nothing of the fact that now I have to get another job, and it isn't easy in the middle of the year. I suppose it's because I built up his ego so nicely, wouldn't you say?" They'd arrived at the school bus. "Why don't you come home with me? You can call your mother."

"All right."

They walked on to catch another bus, a town one, and when they were seated, Betty returned to Mr. Perkins. "How did he do it? What did he say?"

"Oh, he dropped a bottle of cough mixture—he hardly ever drops anything—and he looked so overwrought that I said, Don't you bother with that, Mr. Perkins, I'll clean it up in a second, you get on with the prescriptions, because they're really important. So then he said, Will you marry me."

"But didn't you *expect* anything? Weren't there any preliminaries?"

"I sort of had an idea that . . . that he had ideas. But I wasn't sure. I'd think it, and then tell myself I was crazy. After all, Mr. Perkins . . ."

"Yes. I see what you mean."

"I feel sort of sorry for him, just the same."

"Feeling sorry for him is what got you in the mess in the first place."

"It isn't exactly a mess," Beatrice said tartly. "I do hope," she added, with the immemorial, only slightly hypocritical kindness of a woman who's refused a proposal of marriage, "that he won't be too unhappy."

Betty couldn't imagine Mr. Perkins being happy or unhappy, but felt it would be tactless to say so. "Let's hope not," she agreed.

There were eleven bicycles, four tricycles and two doll carriages in front of the Roman house. By now Betty was so accustomed to this sight on a nice afternoon that she didn't comment as they inched their way through. Neither did she notice any more the bleakness, the near-squalor, of the street where Beatrice lived. It was simply the street where Beatrice lived, and she could never (even had she wanted to) see it again as she had that first day with Clifton long ago.

Gilda and two girls were playing jacks on the porch. Bouncer, splinted and bandaged by Parm and a friend of his—playing doctor—gave them a constricted greeting. Beatrice stopped to reassure herself that he was in no actual danger, suggested that the patient's recovery would be assisted by his being released from his swaddlings and taken for a walk, and beckoned Betty into the house. Woojums was screaming from an upstairs room. Cora and Grandma were drinking tea in the parlor. Jack greeted them as he went out the door with a monkey wrench. He was trailed by Harry, saying plaintively, "I'm not going to help you, am I?"

"Hi, girls," Cora called. "Come on in. Get some cups."

"Where's Mama?" Beatrice asked.

"Somewhere. How are you, Betty? You're looking gorgeous. Take advantage of it."

"How do you mean?" Betty asked, sitting down. "Hi, Grandma."

"She means," said Grandma, "that you can only be a gorgeous teen-ager until you're twenty. Then you have to start thinking of something else to be. Cora was twenty yesterday. She's feeling her age."

"Were you, Cora? I'd have gotten you something if I'd known. You're aging beautifully."

"Aren't you nice. Bea, get some cups. You'd better get some more tea while you're at it."

"Okay. Where is Mama?"

"Somewhere. I said to myself yesterday morning, My girl, you've arrived at a milestone."

"You don't have to carry it around your neck," said Grandma, and crowed.

Beatrice went in search of her mother, and Cora prattled on, ignoring the wails from upstairs that were making Betty uneasy.

"What's the matter with Woojums?" she said finally.

"Oh, he's mad. He's gotten awfully people-conscious and doesn't like to be left alone ever."

"You can leave me alone if you like," said Grandma haughtily. "I'm not one to go where I'm not wanted."

Cora laughed and patted her hand. "Talking about Woojums, dear. Not you."

"I'm not surprised," said Grandma obscurely. She was lucid and vague in such sudden turns that no one but Mrs. Roman ever tried to treat her sensibly. "Why don't you go up and get him?" she said abruptly. "You sit here frolicking while your son cries. Shameful."

Cora got up. "Okay. I just thought maybe he'd go to sleep if I left him alone for a while."

"I'm not sleepy at all, young woman, so don't you try any of your tricks with me."

Cora gave Betty a hopeless glance and started away as Mrs. Roman and Beatrice came in.

"I have to get Woojums. Grandma says."

"He'll be quieter here than he is there," said Mrs. Roman. "Hello, Betty."

"Hi, Mrs. Roman." Betty looked quickly, inquiringly, at Beatrice, who shook her head.

"When Cora comes back," Beatrice said. "Might as well get it all over at once."

"When Cora comes back what?" her mother asked.

"I'll tell you, Mama. Soon as she gets back."

Beatrice moved nervous hands among the teacups, sighed when her sister returned with Vernon, tear-stained and hiccoughingly content, and toyed with the beads at her neck.

"I thought you had something to tell us," Grandma said. "Hurry up and tell us before all the children come back."

"Mama?" said Jack, thrusting his head in the door and recoiling somewhat at the sight of so many females. He had Caruso draped around his neck like a topaz-colored scarf, and the monkey wrench in his hand. "Mama, c'mere."

"Later, Jack, we're busy."

"Right," he said, and withdrew.

"See what I mean?" said Grandma triumphantly. "Next it'll be Harry, and then Parm. . . . Hurry up, Bea."

"I got proposed to today," Beatrice said. She looked around accusingly, defensively.

"Darling!" said Cora. "What fun. But who?" she added in confusion. "You never go out at all, to speak of. I was saying to John only yesterday—"

"Cora," said Mrs. Roman, and her eldest daughter fell silent. "Now, Beatrice. You were proposed to, dear. Who by?"

"Mr. Perkins," Beatrice whispered.

"Mr. Perkins!" Cora shrieked. "He's old enough to be your grandfather!"

"He is not," said Mrs. Roman. "He's a . . . a fine young man." She nodded thoughtfully. "Owns his own drugstore."

"Mama! You're not serious," Beatrice said imploringly.

"Serious? I only said he owned his own drugstore."

"You sounded as if . . . as if you thought it might—"
She was unable to go on.

"I didn't sound any way at all. I said something that happens to be true, that he—"

"Oh, Mama, please. Don't say it again."

"What did you say to him?"

"What do you mean, what did I say? I quit my job. What else could I do? I said I was awfully sorry, but I couldn't marry him and under the circumstances couldn't work for him either. That's what I said."

"Don't get upset, dear." Mrs. Roman exhaled a wistful sigh. "In a way, it's a pity. You've thought it over? You're *sure?*"

"I've thought it over all I need to," Beatrice said coldly. "What do you want, Mama? That I should marry any man who asks me?"

Mrs. Roman, who could be formidable, chose now to ignore her daughter's tone. "No, I don't want that. I suppose I'm just sorry in a way, because a mother likes to see her girls settled."

But not her boys, Betty thought. She felt terribly out of place and wished Bea hadn't asked her along, but could understand why she had. There are times when you need your friends in order to face your family.

"I would never," said Mrs. Roman, "ask you to marry anyone you didn't want to marry. I was only pointing out that he's a nice young man. Not many men his age own their own drugstore."

"If anybody's going to the drugstore," said Grandma, "I'd like an Eskimo Pie."

Cora burst out laughing, and Woojums began to cry.

Later, in the bedroom which Gilda and her friends charitably vacated on Bea's request, the two girls faced each other, waiting.

"Well, anyway," said Betty, not sure how she was going to continue, but sure she should speak, "anyway . . . you've done it. You've got it all said."

Beatrice slumped on Gilda's bed, got up and removed a little sewing kit, sank down again. "I do believe Mama would have been pleased. It's . . . incredible."

"Cora's happy. I suppose she thought you might be, too. Your mother's the sort of woman who thinks marriage is the point, not the man."

"Oh, golly."

There was another long pause. Then Beatrice said, "Still, something like this makes you begin to wonder.

What you *are* going to do, and all. I've just sort of gone along from day to day, supposing the future would take care of itself. But I don't know . . . maybe I'd better do some serious thinking. Before Mama marries me off to someone, I mean."

"You haven't thought about what you're going to do at all?" Betty asked. She hadn't, herself, but she usually figured that with four years of college in view, there was plenty of time. She could start thinking when she graduated.

The real pity, she thought now, is that Bea can't go to college. If the world were correctly ordered, she'd be going, not I. She's the one who loves school, who loves to study, who would find meaning in college beyond what I will. I'm only going—why *am* I going? Because it's expected, because my parents have planned for it, because I don't especially want to do anything else.

"Couldn't you go to college?" she asked. "Get a scholarship, and work? I'm sure you could get a scholarship."

"Maybe I could. The guidance counselor at school thinks so. But you and the guidance counselor don't know my family. Except that you should, by now."

"I shouldn't think they'd stop you if you really wanted to go."

"You don't see," Beatrice said sadly. "Gil can't support the whole family. Cora's husband can't give us any more than he already does. It isn't a matter of stopping me, it's that I wouldn't consider going in the first place. Well, maybe I would in the first place, but not after I thought it over. I wouldn't consider going in the second place, let's say."

"Oh."

It was unbelievably stupid of her, but she simply hadn't thought of that. Gil worked nearly as much as Cliff did. Beatrice had been so busy working after school and on weekends and holidays that she never had time for dates. Jack worked. The Romans needed every hand in order to keep the family going.

"Then what *will* you do?" she asked.

"Oh . . . go to business school, probably. I used to plan ways that maybe I could go to college. I used to think, if Gil wanted to go, by golly Mama would see to it that he went. But that's not really true, I suppose." Beatrice brooded, perhaps not convinced. "Anyway, I quit all that sort of thinking. I mean, it comes under the heading of self-torture, and my New Year's resolution was no self-torture this year."

"You're so awfully pretty," Betty said. "I should think you could be a fashion model. They make lots of money."

Beatrice smiled. "You *are* full of dreams and schemes, aren't you? But, you see, I'm not. I'm a practical person. So I'll go to business school, I guess, and get a job, and someday get married, and I know that's how it's going to be."

But don't you want anything else? Betty thought, a little frantically. Don't you want—or even want to want—something stranger and wilder and richer and fuller? Something different? What was the matter with girls that they settled for so little, with so little fight?

"Why are you looking so rebellious?" Beatrice asked, smiling.

"I'm not sure I can tell you."

"Oh, I'm sturdy."

"I know that. Well . . . it's just that it seems so—well, so tame. So nothing. For someone like you just to sit there and say a job and marriage. Is *that* what life is made of?"

"What else is it made of?" Beatrice asked curiously. "A job and marriage. It doesn't sound tame to me. Who knows what sort of job I might get? As a matter of fact, I have rather fancy ideas about the sort of job I might get. I've been considering being secretary to the first man to build a chain of hotels on the moon. I think I'd like that. Not confining, you know. I'd probably have to make trips from time to time—"

"Oh, Bea," Betty laughed. She did admire this girl so much. Only a year older than I am, she thought, but so much wiser.

"And as for marriage," Beatrice went on, "how you could call that tame, I just don't know."

"Well, it would depend on the sort of marriage, of course."

"Did I specify a tame one? Or—" she grinned "—did you just assume a tame one for me?"

Betty felt bested. She felt that she was showing up in a poor light. "Now I'm confused," she said. "I meant *something*. I meant . . . that I think girls get married just to be married."

"Some do," Beatrice agreed. "But I wouldn't. You wouldn't. Do you ever think about getting married?"

"No," Betty said firmly.

She thought, certainly, about the future. She thought of it in a vague, spangled way, as something that would happen to her . . . sometime. She wasn't afraid of it. She felt, in fact, that it was rather apt to be glorious, above and beyond all matters mundane. But she assigned no place in time to it, no events in particular, and, she realized now with a seeping sense of disbelief and sorrow, she did not people it. Clifton did not figure in her future.

She felt cold suddenly, as if threatened with an unbearable loss. If she never put Clifton in her future, did that mean he was not to be there? That Clifton was to become a man, change and grow and live, and she not be there to know it, to share? What's *wrong* with me? Do I expect to outgrow him, to leave him as part of my girlhood past? Do I think I'm too good for him? *Clifton?* She put her hands to her face and began to laugh.

"Stop doing that," said Beatrice, in a concerned voice.

Betty stopped abruptly. It made her cough. "Sorry. I was . . . thinking of something."

"You'd better think of something else. That was a very unpleasant laugh."

"Sorry," she said again.

They were quiet, their thoughts drifting away from each other.

Betty remembered, with hurtful acuity, worse now than it had been when it happened, the first time she'd seen Clifton in a suit. Always she'd seen him in his tight dungarees, his bright shirts, his windbreaker. It was, somehow, the uniform of Cliff. And then he had asked her to go to New York, to a play. It had been his birthday present to her, in early winter. Clifton had never been to a play in his life, but he thought Betty would like it, and he had got two very good seats for a very sad play because, as he explained to her, "I figured a sad one would be more meaningful." Even meaningful was a word he'd picked up from the Wilders, and somehow it had touched Betty almost to pain. She'd leaned over and kissed his cheek, and said, "I think it's lovely of you, darling. They say it's a very meaningful play." If she'd sounded condescending, she hadn't meant to.

Dinner was to be included, and Mr. Wilder had offered them the loan of his car to drive into the city.

"What a gala evening," Mrs. Wilder had said, as Betty came downstairs. "You look lovely, dear. Very soignée."

Betty had agreed happily. Her mirror had certainly said soignée. Dark blue velvet sheath, pearls, her mother's three-quarter seal, earrings and perfume. She came down in the consciousness that Cliff had never seen her so dressed, that he'd be overcome with admiration for her. Impatiently she waited for him to arrive, waited for the look that was going to be in his eyes when he saw her.

The doorbell rang, and Mrs. Wilder went to answer. Betty and her father waited in the living room, she in a tensely graceful pose that would show off her figure to advantage, her father in his usual mood of quiet resignation when Cliff was due.

Then Cliff came in with Mrs. Wilder and a moment followed that was empty of sound or motion.

Distracted, almost angry with surprise, Betty only noticed at first that he wore his windbreaker. Not a topcoat or overcoat. His everyday checked windbreaker. He took it off with an uncertain gesture, almost with an apology. But he said nothing. He put the jacket down carefully, and smiled. He must have bought the suit years ago, Betty thought. It's too *small* for him. He's outgrown his suit, and he's wearing it anyway. His ankles showed, and his wrists, and he stood there smiling while she wanted to drop with shame. But I can't go to New York with him, she thought desperately. Not dressed this way. One of us has to change, she told herself, fighting back tears.

"Cliff, dear," said Mrs. Wilder (she almost never called him dear, but did so now, protectively), "do you have to leave right away, or have you time for a cup of coffee?"

"Coffee would be great, Mrs. Wilder," he said in a flat voice. The admiration for Betty was in his eyes, but cloudily, as if it had to go through layers of inquietude before it could reach her. "You look beautiful, Betty," he said.

I won't wear the seal, anyway, she was thinking. I'll wear my wool coat, and keep it on during dinner, and hope he doesn't try to take me to a nice restaurant because I won't go. It wouldn't even be so bad, the suit, if he had a *coat*. He'd be sitting down a lot of the time, and the suit wouldn't show too much. Why does he look so magnificent, so dashing, so perfect, in his work clothes, and so . . . so like a *ploughboy*, she thought bitterly, hating herself, when he's dressed the way other men dress all the time?

"Thank you," she said, drawing a deep silent breath that hurt her chest.

Mr. Wilder cleared his throat and seemed on the point of some suggestion, but then he merely offered to make the coffee, and went to do it.

"Perhaps I'd better help him," Mrs. Wilder said. "He bumbles."

"Sure," said Cliff, the slight smile still on his face, as if it were stuck there. "We'll wait." He turned to Betty when they were alone. "Happy birthday, Betty."

"Thank you, Cliff."

"It isn't starting out so happily, is it?"

"I don't know what you mean. It hasn't started at all." And I wish it weren't going to. Could I go up and change into something . . . something not so soignée? How can I go out in this dress with that windbreaker? Oh, how *could* he? She felt chilly and small, and some detached part of her was saying, You feel small because you are small. You don't deserve to love or be loved, since your shame is apparently stronger and bigger than your heart.

"Betty," he said, "I don't have a coat. I never even thought about it until tonight, or I guess I'd have gotten one, but I just don't have one. I never needed one before."

"Never needed a coat?" she said piercingly. "How can you never need a coat?"

"I just never have."

He looked limp. The lines from his nose to his mouth looked deeper. He looked years older than his nineteen, and Betty flung herself against him with a little cry.

"Oh, my darling," she said, wanting terribly to cry, but aware of her parents in the kitchen just beyond. "Cliff, how can you bear me? How do you stand my horrible hateful snobby little soul?"

"I love you, and it isn't a little soul." He held her close, kissed her gently. "What a nice scent. What's it called?"

"Blue Folly," she said, and shivered at a danger past. She'd been awful, she'd deserved to lose him, but she hadn't. She had him still. "Oh, and I do love you," she whispered. "Cliff, I don't deserve you, but I love you. One day I'll lose you, but I love you."

"You deserve everything, and you won't ever lose me." His arms tightened around her, and he said, "It'll be the other way around, I'm afraid."

"No. No, no, no," she said, leaning against him, safe once more. It seemed her whole life this year had been spent getting angry enough at Cliff to lose him, only to fall more deeply in love each time and keep him. "No, not ever." Her face against his shoulder, she added hesitantly, "Cliff, would you mind awfully . . . borrowing one of Daddy's coats? It isn't that I don't love your windbreaker, but—"

He held her off and looked at her steadily. For a sinking moment she thought she'd made another mistake, had hurt him again. Then her heart sprang as she realized he was laughing softly.

"I forget that clothes mean so much," he said. "Well, if your father is willing . . ."

She knew he didn't like it, knew that the laughter was not altogether happy, but he loved her enough to ask for a coat and then wear it. But wasn't I right? she thought now in Beatrice's room, long long after. Could *any* girl wear a blue velvet sheath with a boy who was wearing a windbreaker over an outgrown suit?

"If you loved someone," she said to Beatrice, "would

156

you be able to wear a blue velvet sheath and go out with him if he was wearing a windbreaker and a suit that didn't fit?"

"If I loved him I wouldn't care if he was wearing a space suit and feathers in his hair."

Betty felt suddenly tired.

12

"And so," said Mr. Wilder to his wife, "I said to him, For the money you're paying me, this is the worst I can do. He didn't even see the humor in that, and it's quite a funny remark, made, as a matter of fact, some time ago by Henry James during a period when he was doing articles from France, for the *New York World*, I believe it was."

"Did you, dear?"

"Did I what?"

"Say that to him?"

"Of course I said it to him. I just said I did, didn't I?"

"Don't snarl at me just because Mr. Big of Bigotry doesn't think Henry James is funny."

Mr. Wilder, whose brooding eyes had been fixed on an uneven brick in the mantel (that brick had annoyed him for months), now looked over at his wife with frank pleasure. "Say, that's good. Mr. Big of Bigotry. Is it your own?"

"When I quote, I give credits," she said demurely.

"It's good. I'll use it. You won't mind if I give people to understand it's my own."

"It now is," she said. "All yours. Anything to please you."

"I'm not hard to please." He walked over and poked at the brick. "You know what else I said to him? This *was* my own, and I thought it was sort of funny. See what you think. I said, You insist this fellow's a coming writer. Well, if he's coming, I'm going."

Mrs. Wilder laughed. "Yes, it is funny."

"Hmm. Well, at the time I thought it was," he said wryly. He leaned forward to study the brick. It was firmly in place, but it stuck out. "This thing annoys me. Someday I'll sand it down. Or ask Cliff—" He broke off, went to his chair and sat down. Then he leaned forward a little, hands on his knees, eyes commanding hers, and said with an air of coming to the point, "What I can't stand is the way that boy blows his automobile horn. He sits out there and blows his damn horn and she goes out the door as if it were a summons. He's been in this house precisely once, do you realize that?"

"Yes. I realize it quite well. Joe Preston," she said deliberately, "may not have the advantage of manners. On the other hand, he'll be going to M.I.T."

"How I hate it when you're snide. I hate it more than almost anything else. I never for one minute suggested that a college education was to take the place of fundamental decency."

"Oh, I imagine he's fundamentally decent. He just doesn't have any manners."

"Then why is Betty bothering with him?"

Mrs. Wilder turned her head away. "Because she isn't seeing Cliff, I suppose. Girls usually feel they have to see some boy or other. She's going out with a brash young man that she's trying to forget a quiet one with. Sometimes it works."

"Do you know why she isn't seeing Cliff?" he said in a harassed tone. "Has she said anything to you?"

"She won't tell us anything."

"Why not?"

"Because we're adults. Children never quite trust grown-ups."

"She's eighteen. I don't call that a child."

"But the trouble is, you do. When it suits you. You treat her like a child, and expect her to behave like an adult. You can't have it both ways. This goes for me, too, dear. Not just you. Maybe when we begin to treat her like an adult—maybe I mean when she begins to feel like one, *really*—then she'll trust us, tell us things. We can't make her."

"I thought she was in love with Cliff. I really did think she was."

"Did you give her any reason to think she could tell you that?"

"All I said was—" he told her in a goaded manner "—all I ever said was that I didn't want anybody monopolizing her youth. And I don't. Not George or Cliff or this Preston creep. None of them. She's a kid. Let her have some fun."

"You see? A minute ago you were saying she wasn't."

He slapped his hand angrily against the arm of the chair, then lapsed quickly from anger to perplexity to defeat. "I guess I'm just mixed up. Life's going too fast for me, and I totter along as best I can and lose ground every minute. When she was going with Cliff I wanted her back with George and that gang, and—who was it before George? I objected to George, too, didn't I? And now I want her to drop this Joe College and go back to Cliff. And . . . oh, I don't know what I want."

What he can't seem to grasp, she thought with helpless commiseration, is that what he wants is completely beside the point. He just doesn't seem to get it. And there was no use telling him. He'd only get angrier. This was something he'd have to learn for himself, and he wasn't going to learn it easily.

"When she was going with Cliff," he said meditatively, as if he were summing up a problem, "she acted more grown-up, didn't she? She was even sort of different around the house. More helpful, I thought."

"You thought right," she said dryly.

In the week she'd been going with Joe Preston, Betty had fallen, with a rapidity that was hardly to be believed, into her old evasive indolence. It was all Mrs. Wilder could do to get her to tidy her room, and, as a matter of fact, her mother hadn't asked for more. You can't, she thought, with an insight born of recall (she'd once been in her teens and in love and in misery herself), reach, with a list of daily requests, people who are suffering. You only trouble them more. She did not wish, just now, to have Betty any more troubled than she was. Housework could wait until she was back with Cliff, over Cliff, or not so freshly bereft of Cliff. She felt that it was probably all Betty could do right now to handle her school relationships, be polite (which she was being) at home. All she could do to maintain this false and frozen air of felicity, which was not convincing but was certainly, Mrs. Wilder said to herself, good sportsmanship.

I'm proud of her, she thought. But, of course, she could never say this to Betty. Or, maybe one day, far away, she might. Not now.

"What a pity," she said to her vexed, sad-tempered husband, "that you couldn't have gone on liking Cliff the way you did at first."

"I never stopped liking Cliff," he said quietly. "He's . . . a fine, good person."

"But you thought Betty could do better?"

"That sounds ugly," he defended himself listlessly.

"Forgive me. Only, isn't it sort of true?"

He roused himself. "No. It isn't. It just seemed to me, and it seems to me still, that an intelligent young man would want to get himself a decent education. That's what I object to in Cliff."

"That he doesn't want what you think he should want?"

"Everybody wants a good education," he said patly.

"I don't agree. There are ways of life that don't require education. Formal education, I mean. Clifton will always use his mind. And he seems to know where he's going, what he wants to do. I think you're being too rigid."

"And I think you're being pretty hard on me," he said with an air of desperation.

"Perhaps I mean to be. Oh, well," she said, relenting, "I'm sorry, dear. You have your values and Cliff has his, and it's too bad that Betty got caught in the collision."

"How do you know she did?"

"I don't *know*. I just suspect. But, whether I'm right or wrong, I guess there's nothing we can do about it now."

"Besides," he said, continuing some argument he'd been having in his mind, "you have to admit she's too young to get married."

"It seems to me that you're the only one who's talked about that."

"How do you know what they talked about? I may not *know*, but I can suspect things, too. You said she never told you anything."

"I think she'd have told us if she'd been thinking of getting married."

There was a long pause, and then he said, "She has to go to college."

"Yes."

"What do you mean, yes?"

"I suppose I mean yes."

"You didn't sound as if you did. You aren't thinking she *shouldn't* go to college, are you?"

"I'm thinking . . . that probably there's no better reason why she should than why he shouldn't. I think it will be fine for Betty to go to college. She'll have fun, and learn things, no doubt, and grow. But I don't think it's an absolute basic assumption that there is no other way for her. Some people *should* go to college. Beatrice, for instance. I think that girl should be able to go on with school. She's a student. But for Betty . . . it's really just a standard, isn't it? A way of filling time for girls in a certain income group. Or are you going to say that Betty is a student?"

"I'm not going to say anything," he told her loudly. "Nothing at all, about anything."

The doorbell rang.

"I'll get it," said Mrs. Wilder, when her husband didn't move.

When the horn sounded, Betty had picked up a sweater, given herself an indifferent glance in the mirror, walked downstairs, paused to say good night to her parents, and gone out to the waiting car all in slow motion.

She looked, through compulsion, at that driveway, for that truck, but it wasn't there. It had been, though, on a couple of nights when Joe had come calling. So he'd have seen. He'd know. He didn't care enough to do a thing about it, but he knew.

And what difference does it make to me? she asked herself. I should be glad that he isn't caring, because that means he isn't hurt. And I don't want Cliff hurt. If I have to suffer all the time, day and night, at least it's just my suffering. I love Cliff too much to want him to feel like this.

She said this to herself over and over, and almost—not entirely, but almost—believed it.

What was surprising, what constantly stunned her as the days passed, was how hurt didn't show. Probably her parents suspected something was wrong, but they couldn't be sure. Except for avoiding Beatrice, she was the same as ever around school. She'd cried a lot, but her mouth wasn't swollen, her eyes weren't red. Brush your hair, put on some lipstick, wear a fresh cotton dress and a soft sweater, smile frequently, and Joe here thought he was having a date.

He thought he was out with someone who was listening to him, dancing with him, laughing at his jokes. He thinks he's with somebody, Betty would say to herself. He might as well be shadow-boxing, but he thinks he's out with a girl.

There was nothing really to complain of in Joe. He was neat and handsome, attentive. He had a car and an easygoing way of making conversation. He didn't lunge. She did not for a moment doubt that he planned to lunge, but he was taking his time, and meanwhile was agreeable enough to be around. You have to be around someone, she thought, if only to keep you from thinking. It didn't keep her from thinking, but at least the dancing and the bowling and the having to say "Did you, Joe? That was clever" or "Of course not,

Joe. I don't blame you at all" kept you from concentrating too completely on your thinking, kept you from knowing too clearly what had happened.

She knew what had happened. She had lost Cliff. He was gone from her life. Since that was not confrontable, she avoided confronting it by putting herself in Joe's society. It was a society in which she felt slightly catatonic, but since Joe didn't seem to know it, nobody was embarrassed. And when she was alone she made up silly and frivolous dreams of glory and forced them to occupy her mind. She grew famous, she grew deliciously notorious, she conquered the world and stood with her foot on its neck.

She traversed a stark and utter void, but she kept her eyes straight ahead, maintained a tremulous balance, and . . . traversed it, that was all. Meanwhile, there was Joe. One day he'd decide to lunge, but by that time she'd be gone. She took refuge in the future, the far future and the near. In not too many weeks she'd be in college, and then . . . Oh, then she'd be able to look back at this time with no feeling more sharp than ruefulness, wistfulness. Once I was so much in love, she'd say to herself, but that was long ago, long ago. . . .

". . . there have been authenticated, fully authenticated, stories of pilots chasing queer objects through the sky for great distances. Objects, I mean, not describable by any of our methods, of absolutely *unknown* dimensions and construction—"

"That's interesting, Joe." He must be talking about flying saucers again. He frequently was.

"They've written books about it. These objects, you see, are investigating our earth. There hasn't been any move toward invasion as yet—"

"Why would anything that didn't *have* to get on our world ever want to?"

"Now, Betty. Be serious. Let me tell you one case—"

She sighed and moved restlessly, fearfully, knowing (what she had really known all along) that the anodyne of Joe was not much use, had worn off if it ever had been. She was committed to thinking of Cliff. Angrily, painfully, longingly, sickly, in whatever way—she had to think about Cliff. Joe was an intrusion. I'm not being fair to him, she thought, not caring if she was fair or not. This is the last night I'll see him. This riding around to movies and bowling alleys, this listening to Joe and answering him and smiling at him from time to time (because, after all, he's spending his time and his money on me) when all the time I'm breaking in two, just won't do. Since I have to think of Cliff, and break apart, I can be decent enough to do it quietly at home in my room.

She felt, in a way, a certain peace at giving in. She had to suffer, she had to face unfaceable things. Very well, she'd do it and get it over with. Because you surely did get over these things. Men have died from time to time, and worms have eaten them, but not for love. It wasn't just a saying, it was a truth. Face that. Face the grief, and the loss, and then start recovering. You'll never recover while you're riding tandem with Joe, trying to escape.

". . . personally, I believe in these flying saucers. I believe that at this very moment—"

"I know you do," she interrupted. "Let's go to a movie."

"Okay. Did I ever tell you that Ginny took all my money and then doled it out to me?"

"I don't think you should tell me things about Ginny."

"I couldn't even buy a tie without a pay slip and a written memorandum from her, and half the time I think she consulted Rowena before she'd decide whether a bow tie or a four-in-hand. I said to her once, Are you my girl or my mother? For seventeen years my mother told me what to wear, and then Ginny took over. I didn't even have two weeks in between to handle my own affairs."

"Oh, for goodness' sake. You gave her the money didn't you? She didn't pick your pockets. You probably adored it."

"Come to think of it, I guess you're right. But I'm glad you haven't asked to keep my money for me."

God forbid, Betty thought. She wondered whether to tell him now or at the end of the evening that she'd had it. If she told him now, he'd probably take her home, and then she'd have to explain to her parents. She didn't feel like explaining anything at all to her parents. She wouldn't be able to keep this up indefinitely—evading her parents and Beatrice. I wonder if Beatrice is curious about me, or hurt, she thought. All this week she'd avoided her, not wanting to explain or justify or *talk*. But I can't stay away from her forever. She's my friend, and I need her. Only, just now she could not bear all the reminders that Bea and the Roman household would bring her. And she didn't want to go home early tonight, to face the gentle inquiry of her mother and father.

She'd tell Joe later, just before she left him. He'd be astonished, and probably put out, but he wouldn't grieve. He'd ask himself what in the world was wrong with her, and then forget all about it.

Oh, Clifton, Clifton, how am I going to live without you?

A week ago today she'd gotten up before it was light, and dressed and stolen downstairs quietly (though her parents knew she'd be up, she did not wish to wake them) and opened the kitchen door to Cliff. A heady, exciting hour at which to meet him, an hour when they had to keep their voices low and the lights on, when the smell of percolating coffee was thick and rich, and the taste of it, bitter and black, was strange.

"Have a hard time getting up?" he'd asked softly.

"Oh, no, Cliff. It was fun. I hardly slept for waiting to get up. Is Calvin pleased?"

He grinned. "Couldn't be happier."

They were going to take an early morning ride on Calvin, and have breakfast somewhere away from the house. They were going to spend hours away from home and work, away from everything but each other.

"Will he carry the hamper, too?" she asked. "I made us a lot of nice things last night."

"He'll carry the hamper or I'll know the reason why." He leaned across the table and kissed her. "I'd like to have breakfast with you every morning."

Betty flushed and looked away. In some boys that would have been a suggestive remark. In Clifton it was merely honest, the words meant what they said. Her father had once remarked—quoting some poet—"No man is of value unless he is himself, and knows himself." Clifton, she thought now, is a person of great value. He is himself, always. You can trust him to be himself, not to wear masks or disguises, not to shift—charmingly or treacherously—from one role to another.

"You're always yourself, aren't you?" she said suddenly.

He didn't pretend not to understand. "I expect so. Is that all right with you?" he asked gravely, after a pause.

"I suppose it's the all-rightest thing I've ever known."

A moment passed, quiet as the closing of an eyelid, and when it was past they knew each other better than before.

They went outside, and Calvin came thundering over the dark dewy field to greet them. He stood peaceably while Cliff adjusted the saddle, helped Betty up, handed her the hamper, and then swung up behind her. Holding the reins loosely, he let Calvin take his way across the almost untraveled highway, down along the side of the orchard, along the meadow, over the little bridge and on.

Daybreak came, and except for the foraging of animals, the choiring of birds, it was quiet. The quiet of spring, an intensity of growth that swelled buds and beat the sap along and stirred the earth with soundless violence. Gradually a rose wash filled the sky, glinted on wet plowed furrows, shone on the eastern windows of scattered houses, absorbed a low white drifting mist, and warmed the air so that the smell of things seemed to waken. Smell of grass, of pine needles, of the leather saddle and Calvin's glistening brown hide.

They ambled on, stopping once to watch a large turtle pass. He looked like a casserole with a stalk of endive thrusting out, and he lifted his webbed feet carefully, as though feeling his way.

"I always wonder," said Clifton, "if they know where they're going, or are just on the road, so to speak. If a turtle starts out from somewhere, does he go back, do you think?"

Betty laughed. "I never thought of it."

"Do you want to think of it now? We have plenty of time."

"No. I just want to think about being with you."

Clifton lifted and dropped the reins, and Calvin moved on.

"I used to do this a lot," Cliff said after a while. "Get up early and ride out on Calvin. I wonder what I would have thought if I'd known one day I'd be riding with you."

"Darling, didn't you think you were ever going to take a girl out?"

"Not on Calvin," he said firmly.

I have never been so happy in my life, Betty thought. This is not a day like other days. It is the day that all my life I will remember when I say the word happy. I will remember the sound of the birds and the smell of Calvin and the warm closeness of Clifton's arms next to me. Love was in her like spring sap in a young tree, and she felt jealous and tender and willing. She leaned back against him, rubbing her cheek on his. You're all mine, she told him silently. And I will be yours my whole life long. All my life, all my life, all my life. . . .

"Betty, will you marry me?"

He said it so quietly that she could almost tell herself she hadn't heard correctly. It was what she wanted to tell herself. They were words she didn't want to hear. Go back, go back to a moment ago, she cried in a mute and frightened plea. Go back, Clifton darling, because we were so happy and now something terrible is going to happen. She stiffened quietly, saying nothing, and Calvin moved forward a few paces before Cliff reined him in.

"Let's get off," he said, and leaped down without waiting for her answer. He held up his arms to her, helped her lightly to the ground and released her. She put the hamper down and remained tensely waiting while Cliff loosened the girth on Calvin's saddle. The horse turned his long neck, studied them briefly, and moved off a short distance, cropping the grass.

When Clifton turned to her, his face was so dazzling,

so filled with love and certainty, that she almost moaned.

"Look," he said, drawing her down on the grass beside him, "listen to me, darling. Mr. Perone wants me on his crew. You can't tell what it will lead to, but something big, maybe. Perone's one of the top builders in the state, you know. And he's . . . oh, I don't know how to put it . . . he's an *artist*, if you see what I mean. A guy I'd really like to work with. And this way, it'll be steady work. I mean, long hours still, but just the one job. My mother wants to sell the house and give up the stand, anyway. She's pretty tired. We thought—a smaller house, maybe something closer to town—I mean, I haven't discussed *you* with her, just the part about moving, but—"

"What are you telling me all this for?" Betty cried, and felt as if the sky were falling. What was he doing, with this talk of smaller houses and his mother and . . . any of it? She felt as if he were moving up on her with his house and his mother, as if he were going to clap the whole thing over her and there she'd be—trapped.

Doesn't he understand that we're young, that this is the time to play and talk of love and flirt with wishes and desires that can't be fulfilled for years, and adore doing all that, but not do anything *real*? Doesn't he understand that I haven't been anywhere or seen anything or even *begin* to live? And that he hasn't either? We have so much to do yet, and he sits here talking of marriage. Doesn't he understand *anything*?

"Why am I telling you?" he asked gently, pulling her close. "Because I love you. Because I want you to marry me."

Betty struggled out of his arms and faced him, panting. "I can't marry you, Cliff. I can't. Don't you *understand* that I can't?"

"Understand?" he said slowly. The color drained from his face, and his eyes deepened and glazed. "No. I guess I don't. I thought you loved me."

"I love you, Cliff. I love you with all my heart—"

"People who are in love get married."

"Not people our age, Cliff. There's . . . I have to go to college," she said, and in her own ears it sounded incredible. Trite, insincere. It sounded the sort of thing that you say to get out of a dinner engagement you'd rather not keep. A polite evasion that no one can say is actually untrue.

"Yes. I'd forgotten how much college means in the Wilder household."

"It's a pity it doesn't mean something to you," she said, and gasped. "Cliff darling, forgive me. I didn't mean that."

"Yes, you did. It's . . . all right. It's your father's bias, so how could it not be yours? Only, somehow I thought maybe love would mean more than a few extra years of school."

"It isn't just a few extra years of school. Don't you see that?"

"It's a symbol?"

"Maybe more practical than a symbol," she said, relieved to be a little angry. "I can't understand your attitude about school at all. You don't even care that you never finished high school."

"In my line of work, I don't need it. I've studied on my own. I even think I learn more that way."

"You sound so self-satisfied. Not like yourself at all."

He looked at her tiredly. "Maybe you're right. It's just never seemed . . . I had to go to work, and I never did like school. Maybe you're right. Is this why you won't marry me?"

"Clifton, don't say that. You know that isn't why. I have to say no because I just don't feel ready. Not to think about it, or hear about it—not anything." She put her head down on her knees and began to cry. "We were so *happy*."

"Betty? Betty, darling, don't cry."

He put his arms around her and held her tear-wet face next to his in an embrace that could not comfort either of them. Aching, frightened, miserable for each other, they clung together because they were in love, and because they didn't know what else to do.

I love him, she thought, feeling the rough beat of his heart against hers. I love him, I want him, but I will not say I'll marry him. She couldn't tell him why because she didn't know why. Maybe because she was supposed to go to college, maybe because her father would not approve, maybe because she just felt too young or was too afraid of responsibility. Maybe a lot of things. But not because he hadn't finished high school. Cliff was Cliff himself, the most wonderful person she'd ever known, and how long he'd gone to school could never alter that.

"What it comes to," he said slowly, still holding her close, "is that I love you forever, and you love me but know you're going to stop." His voice was drained of everything but exhaustion.

"It isn't so, it isn't true," she said, crying and unable to stop. "It isn't that at all."

"It's the way you feel about the truck," he went on doggedly. "Oh, I know you love it and love to be with me in it. But you're ashamed of it. Of it, and of me."

"Cliff, don't, don't, don't *say* things like that. You aren't the truck. What if I am a little ashamed of it? You ought to be yourself," she said with a touch of spirit. "It's a wreck. But the truck isn't you. I *love* you, and don't you dare say I'm ashamed of you."

"Then what is it?"

"I don't know. I just don't know."

The long, silent moments lengthened, and then he said, "I'm being unfair. Betty, forget it all, please. Let's go back to where we were. Pretend it never happened, I never said a word. You're right, you're too young." He tilted her chin up, smiled in her eyes, and said again, "We'll go back to where we were."

She swayed in his arms, sniffling, spent, in pain all over. She thought she was probably making the biggest mistake of her life. But it was a mistake she had to make.

They opened the hamper and made a pretense of a picnic. They talked in little spurts that flared and died, but every subject they touched on reminded them of what they couldn't speak of. The morning, which had begun so radiantly, began to cloud over, and far far away, like an augury, one great stone sound of thunder fell down the sky. A breeze rose and carried a sandwich wrapper whirling away from them across the field. Cliff went and retrieved it.

Without consulting, they packed the hamper and prepared to leave. Betty's fingers were unsteady and she pushed things in any way and shut the lid with a jerky, nervous gesture.

This is awful, she kept saying to herself, over and over. It's perfectly awful. It must be how people feel who are getting a divorce. At this thought she burst into tears all over again, crying now with total abandon, utter concentration, ignoring his hand on her shoulder, his voice.

"Betty . . . Betty, my love, please, please forget I ever said anything," he pleaded. "Everything will be just the way it was. I promise you."

She struggled with her tears for minutes, and gradually they subsided. "Do we still have a date tonight?" she gulped.

"Yes. Tonight and every night. Anything you want."

She blew her nose, pushed her hands through her rumpled hair, and got unsteadily to her feet. "I'm sorry. I must look awful."

"You look beautiful," he said, as she had known he would.

Riding back on Calvin, watching the monk-gray storm approach, she told herself that maybe they could, with both of them trying, make things just the way they used to be. . . .

But that evening he neither came nor called.

She could hardly believe it, did not, at first, believe it. Something has delayed him, she told herself when eight o'clock came and went. At eight-thirty her parents went out to a movie, and she could scarcely bid them good-by, so anxious was she to have them gone, to have the necessity of speaking to them, replying to them, over. At nine she was sitting in the living room, a book in her lap, her mind and body alerted for his step on the porch. She was in a passion of waiting that lasted long, because she was so sure. It was just not possible that Cliff would simply fail to show up. Then, when she began to lose hope that he would come, she told herself that he would telephone. He would never, not conceivably, just leave her in emptiness waiting for him.

Restless, bedeviled, unable to concentrate on anything, unable to accept what was happening, she paced the room, sat down suddenly, jumped up again and moved about like a mindless thing caught in a draft. She went into the unlighted kitchen and stared through the night toward his house. The dark shape of his truck was there. There was a light in the kitchen. And a light in Clifton's room. She stared piteously at that lighted square at which she had looked so often, so confidently, knowing that he was there, feeling safe to see the signs that told her so. But tonight? Why was his light on tonight? Why was he there and not here?

"Clifton?" She spoke his name aloud in the empty kitchen. Cliff, what are you doing to me? What are you doing over there?

She sat at the table and buried her face in her arms and struggled with fear and incredulity. He couldn't do this. He just could not. If Clifton just stayed at home tonight (doing what? Doing, for God's sake, *what*? Crossword puzzles? Having a pleasant chat with his mother? What was he *doing?*) just not bothering to call and let her know, even if he had to call and say that he'd changed his mind and they could not go back to where they'd been, if he just stayed home and did nothing and let her suffer, why then . . .

Why then, what? she asked herself, turning her head on her arms, staring with hot eyes out of the window. Then what? Then he wouldn't be Clifton. He'd be some changeable, treacherous, unknown stranger whom she'd taken to be Clifton, whom she'd loved. He'd be a man she'd made up.

Clifton, don't do this to me, she screamed again and again in soundless syllables. *Don't do this* . . .

It was ten-thirty.

She got up, arms hanging at her sides, and walked back into the living room. There were some ashtrays to be emptied. A few papers to straighten. She moved the Venetian blind to a careful adjustment and told herself it should be cleaned pretty soon now. With deliberate cruelty she reminded herself of how she had tried to be a housy person, to be a person to Cliff's fancy. She went over, not step by step, but with glancing hard-heartedness, times that they had had together. Remember that turtle this morning? she asked herself slyly. Remember how everything looked so beautiful with the sun rising? Remember the nights in the truck? Ah, and remember the day he stood in the kitchen and you told yourself you'd never seen anyone you wanted so much to know?

Well, now you know him.

At eleven o'clock she went upstairs. She took a bath, put her hair up, opened the window to the wet, faintly chill spring night, and sank to her knees, staring at that still-lighted window. Across the meadow a train went by in a string of yellow squares, and she could hear the distant swoosh swoosh of cars on the rainy highway.

I'm all right now, she told herself. Because I don't feel anything any more. He's over there, calmly not bothering with me, and so now I know. Knowing makes anything easier. It's the wondering (all the books will tell you that), it's the wondering and hoping that hurt. Knowing is simply a matter of adjustment. Someone you thought was kind is cruel. Someone you thought sensitive is without imagination. No one with imagination could let another person suffer this way. Someone you thought loved you is too thorned with pride to take a refusal, to understand (or even try) why it had to be made.

Well, that's that. Get used to it. This night is a punishment being dealt to you by someone you called Clifton. Only there is no Clifton. He's a man you made up, and you're old enough now to relinquish a made-up man.

Her parents came in, and Mrs. Wilder called through the bedroom door, "Betty? Are you home? I thought you were going out."

"No. We . . . we changed our plans."

"Well . . . would you like some Postum?"

"No, thank you, Mother. Good night. Say good night to Daddy for me."

She probably wasn't fooling her mother. She rarely did. But it was the beginning of her consternation at how you could gloss over pain sufficiently so that you and those around could pretend it wasn't there.

She turned out the light and got into bed. The sheets were cool and made her shiver a little. As she lay, wondering if she'd ever sleep again, the light in Clifton's room went out.

He called in the morning, but Betty, cocooned by an endless, wide-eyed, desperate night, was not moved by his voice at all. She said, "I have nothing to say to you, Clifton, and I've never hung up on anyone in my life before, but I'm going to hang up on you."

When she turned from the telephone, she found her mother at the kitchen door, looking at her in shocked and pitying surprise.

"Anyone for Empirin?" Betty said brightly.

Her mother, on the verge of speech, turned away.

Joe Preston called two days later. It was the third time he'd tried to make a date with her, and she said to herself, listening, that such persistence ought surely to be rewarded.

"There's a cool combo coming to the Golf Club tomorrow night," he said. "How about you and me toddling over there to practice the box step?"

She agreed to go, wondering why he had to talk the way he did.

Her quick acceptance seemed to leave Joe floundering. He'd obviously prepared a sales talk that he now didn't know what to do with. "I was going to say," he began, "that you don't often hear a combo . . . Oh, well. About eight, then?"

"That will be fine."

Joe came into the house that first night. He met her parents as if they were visiting school officials and whisked her out the door. He had taken her out three times since, but had been content to blow his horn and wait, slumped at the wheel, until she appeared.

"Didn't you used to go with Cliff Banks?" Joe said now, as they were driving home.

They had had their movie, their soda, their flying-saucer talk. She was still firm in her decision to tell him this was the last night she'd see him, but had decided to do it right in front of her house. He couldn't argue then. If, that was, he wanted to argue. Considering the sort of company she'd proved to be, chances were he'd be glad to call it quits.

She stiffened now at the sound of Cliff's name. Not with anger, not with awareness of Clifton's cruelty and insensibility, for that flimsy protection had long been stripped from her. She simply didn't want Joe talking about him.

"Hmm?" she said. "Do you think those saucers will ever land, Joe?"

It worked. He rambled on and she retreated to the place where she always was these days, to that void where she had to keep her balance every second.

Whatever had kept Cliff away that night, it was not cruelty or insensibility. Something had happened, and now she'd never know what it was. She'd been too quick to anger, too fierce in her pride, to have any chance of forgiveness or understanding now. We were both confused, she thought sadly. When you're in love, you try to change for the other person, and you try to be true to yourself. Between the two, Cliff and I got so mixed up that we lost each other.

She'd lost him, but could not persuade herself, though she'd tried, that it was a fortunate loss, that she was going to be better for it, once this period was over. And perhaps any man had a right to stay away after being refused in his first proposal. I wouldn't know, Betty thought wearily. I wouldn't know about such things. I only know I love him, and that in some way I'll love him all my life, no matter what happens. I only know that I hope this passes pretty soon, because it hurts too much, and I'm tired of hurting.

If you love someone, she thought, arriving sorrowfully at a piece of knowledge, you *don't* try to change yourself. And you don't try to change him. You take each other as you are. Clifton knew that. Beatrice had told her. But apparently this was something you had to learn yourself, even if you learned too late.

"Joe," she said, interrupting him again (but, then, you had to interrupt Joe or you'd never get to talk at all), "Joe, I really must tell you that this is the last night I can go out with you."

"Huh? Why's that?" He seemed more curious than concerned.

"Because . . ." Why in the world hadn't she thought of something to say? "Because, really, my life is so complicated—"

"I'm not simple," Joe said with a grin. He added, "But maybe it's a good idea, once in a while, to quit while you're behind."

She smiled indifferently. "I'm glad you understand."

"Oh, sure, sure. It's been nice knowing you."

It was the least sentimental leavetaking that Betty had ever had a part in.

Her mother and father were sitting in the living room, in an unmistakable attitude of waiting. Betty stopped in the doorway, looking from one to the other.

"Something up?" she asked warily.

Mr. Wilder cleared his throat and looked at his wife.

"Come in, dear," said Mrs. Wilder. "Sit down."

"All right. What's the trouble? Daddy lost his job?"

"What in the world makes you think that?" Mr. Wilder demanded.

"I don't know. You look funny."

"It's nothing to do with your father, dear. Or, at least, not directly."

Betty's heart took a sudden downward plunge. "Has something happened to Cliff?" she said woodenly. "Has it?"

"No, no, no," said Mr. Wilder, and apparently lost patience. "The boy's fine. He was over here a little while ago, to tell us he's going in the Army."

"The Army? Cliff? What's he . . . what do you mean?"

"You have heard about selective service, haven't you?" Mr. Wilder asked brusquely. He seemed to hear his own tone, and said, "Sorry. I'm jittery. He's been drafted, that's all. Happens all the time."

Betty closed her eyes, opened them, fixed them on her mother. "What happened? Please tell me."

"Well, he came over here, looking for you—"

"Looking for me?"

"That's what he said. And then he told us he'd been drafted."

"But he's supposed to go to work for Mr. Perone."

"That's what he said," Mr. Wilder put in. "But, of course, the Army waits for no Perones. Cliff says he'll do the Army stint and then come back with Mr. Perone. Perone's willing to take him on later, apparently. Did you know they're going to put the house and fruit stand up for sale?"

Betty shook her head, then nodded. "Sort of." Two years, wasn't it? They took you away for two years. Clifton would be gone . . . and gone where? To meet whom? Do what? But away from her . . .

"Did he say anything about me?" she asked humbly.

"He said," her father told her, "to tell you that for reasons you'll understand, he was very tired that day, and he lay down in the evening to rest for an hour and didn't wake up till after midnight. He says he knew I'd be angry if he telephoned then, and you'd be angry no matter when he did. So he waited till morning. And that's all *we* know," Mr. Wilder went on loudly, "except that you haven't seen him since. *We* never get told anything."

Minutes passed, and Betty, trembling slightly, tried to know what it was she felt. Not joy. Something far stiller and deeper than joy. Maybe peace. Peace after torment, rest after the unsheltered passage through a week without Clifton. He was going away, but he'd left a message, he'd come looking for her. Now she could go to him.

But first, she thought, I must tell my parents, because they're entitled to know. She added, Because I want to tell them.

"You see," she began, "that day, last week, when we went on the picnic . . . Cliff asked me to marry him."

"What did I tell you?" said Mr. Wilder to his wife.

Mrs. Wilder began a gesture of protest to him, of appeal to Betty.

"It's all right, Mother," Betty said. "Daddy's going to understand. You both will, because you love me." Her voice was quiet and steady. "I told Clifton no, but, you see, I didn't really mean it. I said I was too young, that I didn't want to think about it. I think he thought it was partly because he hadn't finished school. . . ."

"He says he's going to finish in the Army," Mr. Wilder offered. "He said he'd thought it over and decided it would be a good idea to finish. I suppose that's because of you?"

"Maybe. I don't know. Maybe he's doing it for me. Maybe," she added deliberately, "for you. I hope he's just doing it because he wants to. What I *know* is that I've learned what it is to be without him, and it's not life. I don't want a life that doesn't include Cliff."

"How about all those things you'd planned to be?" her father asked wistfully. "Remember? A Navy nurse, an archaeologist—what were some of the others? You had so many plans."

"I still have plans. They're just different. I don't want those things any more, Daddy. I want a life with Cliff. I want to be married to him. The way," she added simply, "Mother wanted to be married to you."

"What about college?"

"I didn't mean right now. Cliff has to go in the Army and then come back and start learning to be a builder. I'll go to college. I'd like to. But—" she stood up "—someday, I want to marry Clifton. And I wanted to tell you."

"Yes," said Mr. Wilder. "Yes, I'm glad you wanted to tell us."

Betty ran into the kitchen, returned, and said, "His light is still on. Please, I want to go over there, just for a minute. . . ."

"Mrs. Banks won't like that."

"There are lights on all over downstairs. Maybe he's waiting for me. Maybe she won't mind this time, just for a minute, just so I can tell him." Radiantly happy and sure, on her toes to be gone, she waited for her father's nod of release.

She might have gone without it, but he nodded.

When the door had closed behind her, Mr. Wilder got up and went over to the window. He looked at the road, pale in the moonlight.

"She's growing up," he said.

"Grown, I guess," said his wife, coming to stand beside him.

"Happened suddenly, didn't it?"

"Suddenly?" She shook her head.

"She might change her mind . . . about Cliff, I mean?"

"She might."

"But you don't think so?"

"No. She sounds like a woman who knows what she wants."

A deep, wrenching sigh escaped him. "You told me he was the old-fashioned type. You said he'd ask me first."

"He probably knew what you'd say and didn't want to take a chance. He'll come to you now, though."

"As a formality. They'll make the decision."

"We did."

"Yes," said Mr. Wilder.

He looked around the room for a signal, found none, and looked back to his wife. Then the two of them stared out the window at the road down which Betty had disappeared.

About the Author

MARY STOLZ WAS BORN IN Boston, Massachusetts, and attended the Birch Wathen School, Columbia University, and the Katharine Gibbs School in New York. She wrote all during her years at school—verse, essays, stories, and biographies—but stopped writing for a number of years after she left school.

Mrs. Stolz's first book for young people, *To Tell Your Love*, was published in 1950, and since that time she has written thirteen young adult novels (including *And Love Replied*; *Ready or Not*; *Pray Love, Remember*; *Good-by My Shadow*; and *Second Nature*), a story book for children, and two books for adults.

Mrs. Stolz lived for a number of years in Middleton, New Rochelle, and Pelham (all in New York), and now lives in New York City. In stating why she writes for teen-agers, Mrs. Stolz says, "I do not believe young people are more important or more interesting than other people, but their time of life, their climate, is. To me as a writer, anyway."

Format by Mort Perry
Set in Linotype Janson
Composed, printed and bound by The Colonial Press Inc.
HARPER & ROW, PUBLISHERS, INCORPORATED